W9-AVM-803

Poisoned!

Justin slowly walked back out to the kitchen, trying to ignore his nagging doubts. He wasn't thinking too clearly. The idea of closing his math books and going to bed sounded better and better.

But something kept him from doing that. It was like a small voice in his mind kept saying, *Don't go to sleep. Something's wrong...*

It didn't make sense. Why would most of his family's pulses go up while they slept?

Justin felt a cold prickle of fear...

"Mom!" he said loudly. "Mom, wake up!"

Mrs. Hockley moaned once, but didn't move.

He thought furiously about all their symptoms. He knew he'd heard them described before. Where was it?

If only he could think clearly!

Books in the
Real Kids Real Adventures™
series

Real Kids
Real Adventures™

NUMBER

DEBORAH MORRIS

BERKLEY BOOKS, NEW YORK

If you purchased this book without a cover, you should be aware
that this book is stolen property. It was reported as "unsold and
destroyed" to the publisher and neither the author nor the publisher
has received any payment for this "stripped book."

This is an original publication of The Berkley Publishing Group.

REAL KIDS, REAL ADVENTURES #4:
A SCHOOL BUS OUT OF CONTROL!

A Berkley Book / published by arrangement with the author

PRINTING HISTORY
Berkley edition / November 1997

All rights reserved.
Copyright © 1997 by Deborah Morris.
Book design by Casey Hampton.
This book may not be reproduced in whole or in part,
by mimeograph or any other means, without permission.
For information address: The Berkley Publishing Group,
a member of Penguin Putnam Inc.,
200 Madison Avenue, New York, New York 10016.

The Putnam Berkley World Wide Web site address is
http://www.berkley.com

ISBN: 0-425-16086-6

Library of Congress Cataloging-in-Publication Data

Morris, Deborah, 1956-
    Real kids real adventures / Deborah Morris.—Berkley ed.
    p. cm.
    Originally published: Nashville, Tenn. : Broadman & Holman
Publishers, c1994-<c1995 >.
    Contents: 2. Over the edge ; kidnapped! ; Swept underground—
3. Tornado! ; Hero on the Blanco River ; Bear attack!
    ISBN 0-425-15975-2 (pbk. : v.2). —ISBN 0-425-16043-2 (pbk. : v.3)
    1. Christian biography—United States—Juvenile literature.
2. Children—United States—Biography—Juvenile literature.
[1. Survival. 2. Adventure and adventurers. 3. Christian
biography.] I. Title.
[BR1714.M67 1997]   97-5391
277.3'082'0922—dc21   CIP
[B]   AC

BERKLEY®
Berkley Books are published by The Berkley Publishing Group,
a member of Penguin Putnam Inc.,
200 Madison Avenue, New York, New York 10016.
BERKLEY and the "B" design
are trademarks belonging to Berkley Publishing Corporation.

PRINTED IN THE UNITED STATES OF AMERICA

10 9 8 7 6 5 4 3 2 1

ACKNOWLEDGMENTS

Many thanks to heating/air-conditioning expert
Buddy Atkinson for his help with fact-checking
"A Deadly Gas!"

Real Kids Real Adventures™

NUMBER

4

A School Bus Out of Control!

THE LARRY CHAMPAGNE III STORY

ABOVE: Larry Champagne.

"Laar-ry! Mom wants you!"

Clemente Champagne hid a smile as her ten-year-old brother puffed up to the apartment. He'd been playing football with his friend Perry across the street. She waited until Larry was inside, then slipped out the door.

Larry hurried through the house. "Mom?" he called impatiently. "What d'ya want?"

Their puppy, King Mufausa Champagne, bounced along at his heels, barking happily. King looked like a tan, fuzzy bear. They'd gotten him when he was just three weeks old and fed him with a baby bottle until he was big enough to eat puppy food. He didn't know he was a dog.

Dawn Little answered from the top of the stairs. "I'm up here, honey. What's the matter?"

Larry pushed King away. " 'Mente said you wanted me. I was playing outside."

Mrs. Little looked down at him, puzzled. She was pretty, with brown hair that came down to

3

her shoulders. "I didn't call you. Maybe you heard her wrong."

Larry rolled his eyes. "I didn't hear her wrong. She's always doing this to me. *'Mente!'*" Yelling, he raced off to find his sister.

Unable to find her in the house, he dashed back out the front door. The minute he stepped outside, Clemente jumped out of the bushes nearby.

"Gotcha!" she shrieked, grabbing him from behind.

Larry whirled around angrily. His sister let go of him and collapsed, giggling, to the ground. She had a goofy laugh, kind of like: "Hee-hee-hee-*snort!*" Larry tried to glare at her, but she sounded so funny that he started giggling, too. He finally gave up and joined her on the ground.

"Why do you keep doing that to me?" Larry gasped, wiping his eyes.

Clemente giggled-snorted, "It's fun!" After she calmed down a little, she leaned over to hug him. "You're a funny little brother," she said fondly.

Larry shook her off, afraid Perry might see. It wasn't cool to have your own sister hug you. He stood up quickly and dusted off his pants.

Perry walked toward them, tossing the football from hand to hand. "Larry, you gonna play any more?"

"Yeah. Let's go!"

Larry Champagne III lived in St. Louis, Missouri with his mom, sister, and nine-year-old brother, Jerrick, called Jay for short. Larry and Jay both went to Bellerive Elementary. School had just started a few weeks before. Larry was in the fifth grade.

After another hour of football, Larry came back inside the apartment to relax. Jay was sprawled on the living room couch, staring at the ceiling, with King curled up on his stomach. Larry went over and sat down next to his brother.

"What's the matter?" he asked. Jay was almost exactly one year younger than him. Sometimes he was a tattletale, but most of the time he was fun.

"I was just thinking about Dad," Jay said, tickling King's ear.

Larry nodded. Their father, Lawrence Champagne, Jr., had passed away the month before. Their parents were divorced, but their dad always called and came over a lot. Larry felt a sudden pang of guilt for laughing so hard with Clemente. How could he joke around at a time like this?

He patted his brother's shoulder. "I know. I think about Dad a lot, too. But Mom keeps saying to think about what he would want us to do. He wouldn't want us to be sad all the time."

Larry said it as much for himself as for his brother. The last month had been hard for all of them.

They watched TV together for a while, then Larry wandered back to his bedroom. His walls were plastered with sports posters and awards from school, and his dresser was cluttered with trophies. Most had belonged to his dad.

He picked up one of his father's football trophies. It seemed like all the men in their family were winners. They won at football, basketball, baseball, even soccer. His grandfather had coached Little League, and his uncles had their own shelves full of trophies. Larry studied himself in his dresser mirror, seeing a boy with dark brown eyes, short hair and sticky-outy ears. He wondered sometimes if he could ever live up to the rest of the Champagnes.

On Monday morning, Larry woke up to his mother's voice—and a big, fat kiss on the forehead. He grunted and rolled over, rubbing her kiss off on his pillow. What was it with moms and sisters, anyway?

"Get up, sleepyhead," Mrs. Little said with a smile. "Time to get ready for school."

Larry mumbled something, and she left. But five minutes later she was back again, and this time she wasn't kissing him.

"Larry!" she said sharply, sticking her head in his door. "You're going to miss the bus!"

This time a mumble didn't work. Mrs. Little moved into his room like a storm cloud. "Lawrence Champagne! You get up right now or I'm going to sic your brother on you!"

"Okay, okay." Larry sat up sleepily, pretending he was getting up, but as soon as she left, he dove back under the covers again.

The next thing he knew somebody was whacking him on the head. He sat up, fighting the tangled sheets, to find his brother grinning at him.

"Mom told me to get you up," Jay said gleefully. "She's getting mad."

Larry shoved him away. "I'm up. Now get out of here."

That's the way it went most mornings. Sometimes it was Jay who wouldn't get up; then Larry got to go whack *him* on the head. Clemente, of course, got up on time without being scolded. The boys had decided she did it just to make them look bad.

Larry got dressed, washed his face, and went downstairs to eat. King greeted him joyfully at the bottom of the stairs, running in circles and jumping up to lick his face. Larry stopped to hug King and ended up with wads of dog hair sticking to his pants.

"Look what you did!" he exclaimed as he tried in vain to brush off the hair. "You're one hairy mutt, you know that?" King wagged his tail harder and gave Larry his best doggy grin. Larry laughed.

Some mornings Larry and Jay had time to watch cartoons before school, but not today. Larry had barely finished his breakfast before it was time to go.

He and Jay usually walked to the bus stop. It was just down the street, at the end of the block. They were the fourth ones to be picked up every day.

They had only been standing there for about two minutes when the yellow school bus wheezed up and stopped, red lights flashing. The driver, Mrs. Blackman, waited while they got on, then closed the doors behind them. The bus groaned back into gear and chugged off.

Larry held on to the seat backs to keep his balance as he walked to the back. He liked sitting in the very last seat. When Perry got on, he usually came back to sit with him.

As the bus bounced and wheezed from street to street, Larry stared out the window. He found himself thinking about his dad again. Feeling his throat tighten, he forced himself to think about school instead. He couldn't start crying in the middle of the bus!

He was glad when Perry got on at the next stop. His friend quickly slid into the seat beside him.

"How's it going?" asked Perry.

"Pretty good," Larry lied. The bus jerked to another stop, picked up more kids, then started off again. Within minutes, most of the seats were full. After everybody was on, Mrs. Blackman pulled out onto Highway 40. It took about thirty minutes to get to school.

Larry and Perry talked and laughed on the way, sometimes waving as cars passed them on the highway. The bus was so high that they could see down into the cars. Many had food wrappers and other junk thrown everywhere.

"My mom would get us if we made a mess like that," Larry said. "She yells at me all the time about my room, and it's not all that bad."

Perry smiled. "Yeah, but your mom's fun. I loved it that time she snuck up behind you while we were watching TV. You jumped about a mile."

Larry laughed. "She does stuff like that all the time . . . tickles us and runs off, or chases us all around the house. She's goofy, like my sister."

By the time they reached Bellerive Elementary, Larry was feeling much better. Having other people around helped take his mind off his own problems.

Larry and Jay were both tired and hungry when they got home that afternoon. King met them at the door, barking and wagging his tail. They stopped and played with him for a minute, then made a beeline for the refrigerator.

Clemente was busy washing dishes. Since middle school let out earlier, she always got home before them.

"Hi!" she said brightly. "I saved the last couple peanut butter cookies for you if you want them."

"Thanks!" said Larry. 'Mente might play a lot of tricks on them, but she also looked out for them. On Valentine's Day, she had cooked a special dinner for the whole family. She had even made Kool-Aid and served it in wine glasses. She was a lot like their mom.

After wolfing down the cookies, the boys went to do their chores. All three kids took turns doing the dishes, cleaning the bathroom, and vacuuming and dusting the living room. Since Clemente had already done the dishes, that left the bathroom and living room for them.

"I guess I'll take the bathroom today," Larry said. "You can do the living room."

King followed Larry into the bathroom and

watched curiously as he sprinkled Comet into the sink and started scrubbing. Larry knew better than to do a sloppy job. When his mom said to clean something, she wanted it to *sparkle!*

When he finished, Larry turned to the dog. "You want to play, boy?" he asked. King had a way of staring and looking pitiful if you ignored him. The whole time Larry had been cleaning, King had been drilling holes in his back with his eyes.

Now, hearing the word "play", the puppy bounced around happily. Larry wrestled with him for a few minutes, then ran upstairs. King followed.

They kept a trampoline upstairs. It was a small, one-person (or one-dog) size. King loved to jump on it.

Larry stepped onto the trampoline and bounced a few times, then jumped off. Instantly, King jumped on. He got in one or two good bounces on the trampoline before he fell off. It was hard for him to keep all four legs on the round rubber part. They took turns bouncing until Larry got tired.

"Sorry, boy," he said, panting. "I've got to do my homework now. You'll have to go play with Jay."

King tilted his head like he was listening, but he looked disappointed when Larry started back downstairs. If King had his way, the whole family would do nothing but play with him all day.

Larry was sitting at the kitchen table struggling with an English worksheet when Clemente walked in. She looked over his shoulder and sniffed.

"That's so *easy*," she said. "You ought to see the stuff they're making *us* do now."

Larry ignored her. She watched him for a moment, then said, "You want me to show you how to do that?"

"Sure," Larry said gratefully. He slid his paper over so she could see it better. "I always get confused about nouns and verbs."

"I'll show you." Clemente sat down next to him and took his pencil. With a few quick strokes, she erased what he had done and brushed the little eraser "worms" off onto the floor.

"Now," she said firmly, "all you have to remember is that nouns are *people, places*, or *things,* and that verbs are *action* words."

Larry yawned. She sounded just like his English teacher. Clemente looked at him through narrowed eyes.

"Are you listening to me?" she demanded.

"Um-hum." Larry leaned his face against his hand and blinked a few times. People. Action. Why did they have to make English so hard?

"Okay. So in the sentence, 'Sharon ran to the store', what would the action word be?"

"Ran?" Larry guessed.

Clemente beamed at him. "Right! Now this is harder. What's the noun?"

Larry sighed. People were nouns, right? "Sharon," he said.

Clemente looked sly. "Is that all . . . ?"

"I guess so. You *said* people were nouns!"

His sister nodded with a superior air. "But I also said *places* and *things* were nouns. 'Sharon ran to the *store*.' You get it?"

Larry's brain felt tired. "Yeah. Store is a noun, too."

Clemente slid the paper back in front of him. "Okay, now you do the rest."

Larry took back his pencil and worked his way down the page, underlining nouns and circling verbs. Clemente was good at English, so he supposed she knew what she was doing. He didn't let her help with his math homework anymore, not since she'd "helped" him get a D on one paper. That had made him mad. He liked getting good grades.

Mrs. Little got home at five-thirty. She worked as a Service Rep. for the local phone company. "Hi, kids!" she called out when she walked in. "I'm home!"

Larry, Jay, and Clemente all ran over to hug her. They knew the last few weeks had been hard for her, too. She looked tired.

"How was work, mama?" Clemente asked.

"It was fine, honey." Mrs. Little threw her purse onto the couch and sat down next to it. "I'm not much in the mood to cook tonight, though. Does pizza sound okay to everybody?"

"Sure!" they chorused. They ordered pizza so much that the local Domino's Pizza people recognized their voices. When Clemente called, they asked if she wanted the usual: a sausage pizza on the original crust. She said yes.

Thirty minutes later, the pizza arrived. While

Mrs. Little paid for it, the three kids raced to the kitchen table. They had three good chairs and one broken one that wobbled. The last kid to the table every night got stuck with the wobbly chair. Their mom always got a good chair.

Larry was last this time. Balancing on the wobbly chair, he attacked the hot, cheesy pizza with shark-like bites.

"Did anything interesting happen at school today?" asked Mrs. Little.

Larry swallowed quickly. "On the bus home, Mrs. Blackman gave us all assigned seats. She's gonna make me sit right in the middle from now on."

"Did you ask her why she was assigning seats?" Mrs. Little asked.

"Yeah. She told me to stop asking her so many questions."

Clemente smiled. Larry was always asking "Why this?" and "Why that?" Until he understood the reason for something, he could be as stubborn as a mule. Poor Mrs. Blackman would've been better off explaining it to him!

"Well," Mrs. Little said sympathetically, "God has a plan in everything, Larry. And it won't kill you to sit somewhere different for a change, will it?"

"I guess not," Larry said grumpily.

The next morning was dark and rainy. Larry made a face when he looked outside. He didn't feel like standing in the cold rain waiting for the bus, especially when he'd have to sit in his stupid assigned seat. Maybe he could talk his mom into driving them to school.

Mrs. Little was getting ready for work when Larry started in on her. "Mama, can you drive us to school today? It's raining!"

His mother glanced outside. "It's just drizzling, honey. And your school is in the exact opposite direction of my work. I'd be late if I drove you in first."

Jay was listening. "Ple-e-ase?" he chimed in. "It's *raining,* mama." Since he was the youngest, he could sometimes talk her into things by looking little and cute.

Not this time, though. "Sorry, guys," Mrs. Little said. "You need to get on the bus. But I'll tell you what—I'll drive you to the bus stop and let you sit in the car until the bus comes. That way you'll stay dry. Okay?"

Larry sighed. "Okay," he said unhappily. "I just wish we could sit where we want. These new rules are dumb."

It was almost seven o'clock when they ran out to their mom's Ford Taurus. Larry beat Jay to the car, so he got to sit in the front seat.

Mrs. Little drove them to the corner and stopped, leaving the motor running. Larry decided to give it one more try.

"Mama, can't you drive us to school just this once?" he begged. "I really, really don't want to ride the bus today."

"Will you stop it?" Mrs. Little said in exasperation. "I know you don't like having an assigned seat, but that doesn't mean I'm going to drive you to school every day. You're riding the bus, and that's it. Got it?"

"Yes, ma'am." Larry slumped back in his seat. When the bus pulled up he got out and trudged over to it, not caring that the rain was making splotches on his clothes. He paused at the door to wave good-bye to his mother, then followed Jay up the steep metal steps.

Larry ignored Mrs. Blackman. He had liked her until she got the idea of assigning seats. Still, she wasn't as bad as some of the other drivers who spent all their time yelling and glaring at the kids.

She waited until Larry started down the aisle, then closed the doors and put the bus in gear.

Jay's assigned seat was right behind Larry's. Larry tossed his book bag onto the seat and sat down, his arms crossed. He became even gloomier when they reached Perry's stop. Perry wasn't there. *His* mom had probably driven him to school so he wouldn't have to sit in a stupid assigned seat.

Larry sighed and looked out the window, watching the rain. The noisy chatter inside the bus increased as more and more kids got on. There were nineteen children on board when Mrs. Blackman finally turned onto the highway.

This part of the ride always made Larry sleepy. The sound of the tires humming and the wind leaking through the windows lulled him. If the seats weren't so hard he'd take a nap.

He wiggled in his seat. The bus was going fast now. Several fancy cars with radar detectors blasted past them, going about ninety. Larry idly glanced around the inside of the bus, then up at the bus driver.

That was when it happened.

As he watched, Mrs. Blackman looked down— then slowly fell sideways, her hands still gripping the steering wheel. Larry's mouth flew open. Before he could move, the whole bus swerved to the right. His book bag shot off the seat onto the floor, and he was thrown halfway out into the aisle. A chorus of shrieks went up as other kids slid out of their seats.

Larry stared in disbelief at Mrs. Blackman. She was almost upside down, her head pointing down toward the steps. Only her seat belt kept her from falling the rest of the way out of her seat. As the bus veered wildly across the busy highway, Larry scrambled to his feet, heart pounding. Horns blared and tires screeched as cars swerved to keep from slamming into them. The kids screamed in terror. They were going over fifty miles per hour with no one at the wheel!

Seconds later the bus hit a steel guardrail on the right side of the highway. The bus tilted, sending Larry flying sideways. He landed on top of several other kids. By now they were all screaming and sobbing. For a moment it felt like the whole bus was going to roll over; then it bounced off the guardrail and veered back across the highway.

Larry crawled over the other children and stood up again. He had to do something! He had to stop the bus somehow, or they were all going to die.

The middle aisle was jammed with a tangle of kids, books, and lunch boxes. The younger kids were all wailing in terror. Larry jumped over them, racing for the front of the bus.

He was almost there when they slammed into the guardrail on the other side. Once again he went flying, this time hitting his back against the steel bar behind the driver's seat. It hurt, but he didn't have time to think about it.

He had to stop the bus.

Mrs. Blackman wasn't moving. Larry dodged around her, trying not to step on her. She was all the way out of her seat now, lying on the floor by the steps. Larry caught one glimpse of her open, staring eyes, and goose bumps prickled his arms and neck. She looked dead!

But he didn't have time to panic. There were no other adults on the bus, nobody else to do anything to help them. It was up to him.

Grabbing the steering wheel, Larry hauled himself into the driver's seat. Between the kids' screams and all the horns honking, his eardrums felt like they were going to burst. His heart was pounding so hard that it felt like *it* was going to burst, too. He had never been so scared in his life.

The bus zig-zagged across the busy highway, heading for the right guardrail again. Larry hauled on the wheel, trying to turn the bus back to the left. He had to haul the wheel almost all the way around before the bus turned even a little.

The brake. He had to find the brake.

Feeling around with his right foot, he found the pedal. He gripped the steering wheel harder and stomped the pedal with all his strength.

The sudden braking flung him forward. His forehead bashed into the windshield. Behind him the screaming grew louder as the other kids started sliding forward.

Dazed, but still determined, Larry kept his foot planted on the brake. The bus was turning too far to the left now, so he jerked the wheel back to the right again. They were finally slowing down. In another few seconds the bus would be stopped.

Something crashed into them from behind. Larry almost lost his grip on the steering wheel. The screams and sobs inside the bus became frantic shrieks. Larry couldn't turn around to see what was happening, but in the bus' outside mirror he saw a small pickup truck right behind them. As he watched, its back wheels bounced up off the ground a few times. The front of the truck must be jammed into the back of the bus!

The bus sputtered a few more times, then stalled. It rolled and jerked to a stop in the middle of Highway 40.

Larry slowly let go of the steering wheel. His hands ached from squeezing the wheel so hard. All the noise—the kids sobbing, the horns outside—suddenly seemed far away. He flexed his fingers, feeling like he was in a bad dream.

Then he remembered the bus driver. He couldn't leave her lying there like that. He knelt next to her and tried to lift her by her shoulders, but she was too heavy. He couldn't bring himself to look at her face.

He was still squatting there beside her when a man ran up and banged on the bus doors. Larry used the handle to swing open the doors.

The man ran up the stairs, almost stepping on Mrs. Blackman. It was the driver of the pickup truck that had hit them.

"Is everybody all right?" he asked in a panicked voice. Most of the kids were moving back to their seats. "I couldn't stop in time!"

When the kids didn't answer, Larry took over. "Hey!" he shouted, cupping his hands around his mouth. "Is everybody okay? Jay, are you okay?"

Hearing a familiar voice, most of the kids looked up. Jay waved from his seat. "I'm okay, Larry," he answered in a shaky voice.

Seeing his brother alive and well made Larry suddenly feel weak. So many bad things had happened lately. Now, for a change, something good had happened. They'd made it!

The same idea seemed to strike the other kids at the same moment. The crying stopped like it had been switched off. Into the sudden silence, one boy shouted: "Larry saved us!"

Instantly all nineteen kids on the bus took up the chant: "Larry saved us! Larry saved us!"

Larry felt like crying. He tried to swallow, but there was a huge knot in his throat. He stared at his schoolmates, speechless.

Behind him, the man from the pickup truck was using the CB radio to call for help. "The driver is alive," he said loudly, speaking into the radio, "but it looks like she's had a stroke or something. We need an ambulance."

Larry turned around in surprise. Mrs. Blackman was alive? He looked down at her, less scared this time. Her eyes were still open, but he could see now that she was breathing. She *was* alive!

Suddenly Larry wanted to be with his brother. He ran down the aisle to Jay's seat and threw his arms around him. Jay hugged him back fiercely.

"I'm glad you're okay," Larry said.

"I'm glad you're okay, too." They looked at each other, both thinking the same thing. Their dad might be gone, but they still had each other, and Clemente, and their mom. For now, that was enough.

An ambulance took Mrs. Blackman to the hospital, and soon another bus came to pick up the kids. Larry and Jay sat in the back and talked quietly. What had happened still didn't seem real.

They got to school late, but other than that, it was just like any other school day. That afternoon the substitute bus took them home. Larry wondered what had happened to Mrs. Blackman, but he didn't want to ask.

It wasn't until late that afternoon, when his mother got home from work, that Larry learned that some people were calling him a hero.

"I got a message from your principal today," Mrs. Little said after she hugged everybody. "I thought at first that you'd gotten in trouble at school or something. But when I called him back he told me you'd helped stop the bus this morning when your driver passed out. He said you were a hero!"

"It was no big deal," Larry said in embarrassment.

King was circling Mrs. Little's legs, wanting her to pet him. Jay had put Larry's sunglasses on him, so he looked like a movie star dog. Larry laughed.

"Well," Mrs. Little said, "you must've done *something,* because a newspaper reporter called right after that and asked me a bunch of questions. I told him I didn't know much about what had happened. What *did* happen, exactly?"

Larry shrugged. "Nothing much. What's for dinner?"

His mother slapped her forehead. "Oh! I meant to get the roast out of the freezer this morning to thaw, but all your griping about riding the bus distracted me. Now we're going to have to find something else to eat."

Just then, the phone rang. Mrs. Little answered it, listened for a moment, then turned around to look at Larry in amazement.

"Yes . . . Well, I'll have to ask him and call you back. I will. Thanks."

She hung up the phone carefully and turned to look at the kids again. "Do you know who that was?" she demanded. "That was a reporter from Channel 8. They want to come here and put Larry on television!"

Larry's eyes grew wide, but she didn't give him a chance to talk. "Lawrence Champagne, I want you to sit down right now and tell me the whole story. What did you *do?*"

It was eight o'clock that night by the time the TV crew left. Larry had begged his mom to tell the Channel 8 people no, but she had talked him into doing the interview.

"If you were brave enough to stop that bus, you're brave enough to talk to a little camera," she told him. "It's not every day we have a hero in the family!" To celebrate, she let him pick whatever he wanted for dinner afterward.

Larry didn't hesitate. "Pizza," he said firmly. "And chips. And soda." The Domino's people were surprised to hear from them again so soon, but they sent a sausage pizza—original crust—right out.

After dinner, the whole family sat up and waited for the ten o'clock news on Channel 8. When Larry's face came on the screen, they clapped and cheered. Larry just shook his head. He couldn't believe everybody was making such a big deal out of what had happened. Anybody could have done what he'd done.

It was then that he remembered looking at all his father's trophies and wondering if he could ever live up to his feats. But his dad had never made a big deal out of winning; he had always said the important thing was to do your part.

Larry buried his face in King's soft fur, thinking. What would have happened if his mom had given in that morning and driven him and Jay to school? Would somebody else have run up there and stopped the bus?

Probably not.

He had done his part. And suddenly, Larry was sure his dad knew all about it.

Larry Champagne received a "Proclamation of Heroism" from the Governor of Missouri, who came to Bellerive Elementary School to present it to him. He also received plaques from the bus company, a local church, and a number of other organizations honoring him for his quick actions.

Larry, Jay, Clemente and King.

A Burning Ship!

THE JENNY PETERSON STORY

ABOVE: *Achille Lauro* on fire.

Jenny Peterson wrinkled her nose at her reflection in the mirror. Her uniform from Overwaitea Foods could make a supermodel look fat. She turned sideways, flipping her thick brown braid over her shoulder. As usual, the lumpy blue shirt puffed out in back, making her look like a hunchback. She might not be a super-model with her brown eyes and slightly pudgy cheeks, but she was no hunchback, either!

Well, Jenny told herself, *this uniform is one thing I won't miss when I leave!*

This was the seventeen-year-old's last day of work at the local grocery store in Burns Lake, a small Canadian town in British Columbia. At the end of her shift, she quickly changed into black jeans and a red sweater, then went out to tell everybody good-bye. She would miss her friends, but it wasn't every day she'd get a chance to work on a luxury cruise ship! She still couldn't believe her good luck.

Jenny shivered as she hurried across the parking lot to her car. In early November it was already cold and snowy in Burns Lake. Jenny had dreamed for weeks of all the sunshine she would soak up once she was on the *Achille Lauro,* cruising on tropical seas.

Driving home, she went over her travel plans for the thousandth time. Had she forgotten anything?

Her plane tickets were ready. Next week she would fly to Germany, then on to Italy, where the ship would be waiting. The tickets had cost her a fortune, but it would be worth it. Six whole months on a cruise ship, and all she had to do was baby-sit a few kids. How hard could that be?

Had she packed everything she'd need? Her biggest suitcase was jammed tight with all the new clothes she had bought. She'd even managed to squeeze in her DiscMan CD player, about twenty CDs, and enough makeup to sink a ship.

Well, maybe not that *much,* Jenny thought with a smile. But six months was a long time to be gone. She didn't want to run out of makeup and scare people.

The shipping company, Starlight Cruises, had sent her a list of things to pack. For the "formal night," she had packed her almost-new high school graduation dress. It was made of satin and black velvet, and had big, puffy sleeves. She had boxed up all the other things in her room so Juline, her fourteen-year-old sister, wouldn't get into her stuff while she was gone.

What else? She had gathered all her friends'

addresses so she could write to them. She had quit her job at Overwaitea Foods. And last, but not least, she had broken up with her boyfriend, Dave.

Jenny shook her head, remembering how Dave had exploded when he learned she had taken the job on the *Achille Lauro*. He hadn't liked the fact that she would be gone for six months. After talking it over, they had agreed it would be best to break up and just be friends.

Jenny yawned. She had been so excited about the trip that she hadn't slept well for weeks. She would be glad when it was finally time to leave. Maybe then she could relax!

Pulling into the driveway at home, she saw several strange cars parked outside. Her mother must have friends over. It was Sunday afternoon, so maybe she had invited them for dinner. Jenny hoped she wouldn't have to help entertain them. She was tired after working all day.

Jenny walked in and hung up her coat. "Mom, I'm home!" she called. No answer. She started into the living room, wondering where everybody was. What she saw stopped her cold.

The living and dining rooms had been transformed into a Christmas Wonderland. Popcorn strings, balloons, and Christmas decorations were strung from wall to wall. A tall houseplant had been turned into a miniature Christmas tree. It even had presents stacked under it!

She was still staring, speechless, when a crowd of family and friends jumped out to shout: "Merry Christmas, Jenny!"

Suddenly squashed from all sides by hugs and kisses, Jenny looked around for her mother. She spotted her off to one side, beaming. This must have been her idea.

Once she caught her breath, she fought her way through the crowd to her mother's side. "What's going on, Mom? Isn't it a little early for Christmas?"

Ms. Peterson smiled. "You won't be here for Christmas, so we just decided to move it up a little. Come get something to eat. Then you've got presents to open!"

Laughing, Jenny followed her over to the dining room table. It was heaped with party food. She fixed a plate, then wandered around talking to everybody. Many of her friends from school and work were there. How had they arranged all this without her finding out?

Opening the presents was a lot of fun. She got a huge black teddy bear from her mom. "It's to guard your room while you're gone," her mother explained. Jenny laughed.

Several friends-gave her pictures from graduation

CLOCKWISE FROM BOTTOM: Ms. Peterson, Juline, and Jenny.

night to remember them by. Then Juline handed her a small package.

Jenny smiled at her sister, a little surprised. Juline had been acting jealous lately of all the attention Jenny had been getting. She tore open the wrapping to find a tiny, perfectly crafted glass Christmas tree.

"It's small enough so you can take it along," Juline said nervously. "I thought you might like to have something Christmassy around on the real Christmas."

Jenny grabbed her little sister in a big hug. "I love it! Thank you so much." Juline hugged her back, hard. For the first time, Jenny realized how much she was going to miss her family. She'd never really been away from home before for more than a few days. This might be harder than she thought!

The next week flew by. On the morning she was to leave for the airport, Jenny ate a big breakfast with her mom and sister. Juline wanted to come along when Ms. Peterson drove Jenny to the airport, but it was a school day. Juline and Jenny had to say a tearful good-bye.

Jenny was quiet on the way to the airport. Now that the time had finally come, she was having second thoughts. She knew her mother hated the idea of her going so far away, even though she'd tried to hide it.

I'm already homesick and I haven't even left yet, Jenny thought with a sinking heart. *How will I stand being gone for six months?*

It wasn't until she reached her gate at the airport, though, that Jenny lost it. She suddenly dropped her suitcase and flung herself into her mother's arms.

"I've changed my mind, Mom!" she sobbed. "I don't want to go!"

Ms. Peterson hugged her tight. "Oh, honey, I don't want you to go either, you know that," she said helplessly, patting her back. "But the tickets are already bought, and the shipping company is expecting you. You can't just not show up."

"Can't you come with me, then?" Jenny begged. "I've never flown on a big jet before, and I have to change planes in Germany. I don't know how to do this stuff!"

Ms. Peterson patted her back soothingly. "You'll do fine. People will be at the airport to help you. And once you get on the ship, you'll probably never want to come home! Everything will be just fine, you'll see. It'll be an adventure."

Her words gradually calmed Jenny. When the announcement came that it was time to board the plane, Jenny took a deep breath.

"Well, I guess this is it. I'll write every chance I get."

"Me too," Ms. Peterson said. "Just be careful, okay?"

"Okay. I love you, Mom."

Grabbing her suitcase, Jenny joined the long line of other passengers shuffling onto the plane. Her adventure had begun.

Over twenty-four hours later, an exhausted Jenny stepped off the second plane, still lugging her heavy suitcase. Her first flight had taken nine hours to reach Germany. Now she was in Genoa, Italy, where somebody from the ship was supposed to meet her at the gate. She glanced around, wondering how she would recognize whomever it was. What would happen if they didn't show up? She couldn't speak a word of Italian!

Then she saw a woman holding up a sign that said: "Jenny Peterson." Relieved, Jenny quickly shoved her way through the crowd, trying not to knock people down with her suitcase. It felt like it was packed with bricks. Why had she brought all that junk?

"I'm Jenny Peterson," she said breathlessly when she reached the woman. "Are you from the ship?"

"Yes. My name is Christina. Starlight Cruises sent me to meet you." The woman spoke with a crisp South African accent, somewhere between a British and Dutch accent. Jenny thought it sounded pretty.

Just then, a young man joined them. He held up another sign with a grin. It also said "Jenny Peterson."

"Somehow they ended up sending two of us to meet you," he explained. "Guess they wanted to make sure you got to the ship, huh?"

"I'm glad," Jenny admitted. "I was just wondering what I was going to do if nobody was here to meet me."

"Well, you're probably tired after flying halfway across the world. We've got your cabin ready for you aboard the *Achille Lauro.* The docks are only about twenty minutes away."

It was late at night as they drove through the streets of Genoa. When they reached the docks, Jenny stared at several sleek passenger ships gleaming in the moonlight. It hardly seemed real. She, Jenny Peterson, was in a foreign country, looking at glamourous ships from all around the world. And soon she would be on one!

When the car stopped, though, it was in front of a huge, square ship that looked like it was still under construction. Jenny's heart sank. The vessel was strung with work lights and draped with sheets of paint-spattered plastic. Boxes, paint cans, and stacks of lumber were scattered around the deck. It looked cold and bare, more like a metal prison than a glamourous cruise ship. This was the *Achille Lauro?*

"Here we are!" Christina said cheerfully. "Don't mind the mess; we're just finishing a multi-million-dollar renovation. New carpet, new paint, the works. By the time we leave it'll look like a new ship."

I sure hope so, Jenny thought silently. The idea of spending six months on that ugly metal crate petrified her. What had she gotten herself into?

Walking up the gangplank a few minutes later, though, she felt a thrill of excitement. The air had a wild, salty-fishy smell, and she could hear the water slapping the side of the ship. So what if the *Achille Lauro* wasn't quite like she had imagined? This was still an adventure, and she was going to enjoy every minute of it!

She followed Christina across the main deck, then up three flights of stairs. "You're in Cabin P-123," Christina explained. "You can put your things away, then I'll take you down to dinner."

The ship's hallway was lined with rows of doors, just like in a hotel. When they reached Cabin P-123, a tall, blond woman opened the door. She was wearing a swimsuit and cover-up. Jenny stared; with her perfect hair, perfect face, and perfect figure, she looked exactly like a big Barbie doll!

"Hi, I'm Sharon," the Barbie doll said with a smile. "Come on in. You must be my new room-mate."

Jenny squeezed through the narrow doorway. The cabin was *tiny,* like a large walk-in closet with two sets of bunk beds. How many people were supposed to fit in here?

"I'm Jenny," she replied, trying to hide her dis-may.

Sharon grinned. "Don't worry. It feels a little cramped in here at first, but you'll get used to it. You won't spend that much time in here, any-way."

Jenny threw her suitcase on one of the lower bunks. A cabin on a cruise ship had sounded so romantic, but this looked more like a prison cell. What next?

She found out when they went down to dinner. As Sharon led the way deeper and deeper into the ship's belly, Jenny noticed a funny smell in the air—kind of like rotting meat. The further down they went, the smellier it got. Finally, after going down what seemed like 20,000 stairs, they reached a long, skinny hallway. Several large brown bugs were scuttling along the walls and floor.

"Eew!" she shrieked as one of them darted across her foot. "What *are* those things?"

"Cockroaches," Sharon said matter-of-factly. "You might as well get used to them. They're everywhere. They love tropical climates."

Jenny shuddered. She had never seen a roach before. In Canada, it was too cold for them. She walked slowly, trying to look everywhere at once. She didn't like bugs.

She ate dinner in a daze, feeling stupid and out of place. She was the youngest one on the Starlight Cruise staff, and the only one from Canada. She slumped in her seat, trying to hide her colorful Canadian tee shirt. She was proud of her country, but right now she wished she could blend in with the others.

This is an adventure, she reminded herself weakly. She speared a stringy piece of meat and forced herself to taste it. The fancy chef wouldn't arrive until the passengers did; until then, they had to eat whatever the ship's crew cooked. The meat stuff wasn't too bad. She cheered up a little. So far she had met new people, new foods, and new bugs. Wasn't that what adventure was supposed to be about?

After dinner, Sharon and Jenny went back upstairs to look at their uniforms. Jenny pulled the first one out of the closet: a blue-and-white striped skirt with big gold buttons, and a matching striped tank top. She bit her lip. Starlight Cruises must use the same uniform designer as Overwaitea Foods!

"Pretty bad, aren't they?" Sharon giggled. "But

we don't have to start wearing them until the passengers arrive next week."

"Good," Jenny said, shoving it back into the closet. "I think I'll just wait until then to look at the others."

She poked around the small cabin to make sure she hadn't missed anything. Besides the bunk beds and two tiny closets, there was a nightstand and a bathroom the size of a gym locker. The shower looked ancient, with the same old-fashioned "hot" and "cold" knobs she imagined had been used in the showers aboard the *Titanic*. How old was this ship, anyway?

She unpacked her suitcase, carefully taping all the pictures she'd brought to the wall above her bunk. The little Christmas tree from Juline went on the nightstand. She smiled up at her sister's picture on the wall. The tiny cabin already felt more like home.

Before bed, she met her fellow "children's host," a tall twenty-year-old named Dean. Jenny was relieved to learn that Dean had a lot of experience with children.

"I was the NesQuik Bunny for a while," he admitted ruefully. "I wore this big pink bunny suit and patted kids on the head. They loved me." He promised to show Jenny the ship's playroom the next day. They were supposed to decorate it before the passengers arrived.

As Jenny drifted off to sleep that night, her thoughts were in a pleasant jumble. Nothing had turned out quite the way she had expected . . . but that was okay. It looked like this job might turn out to be fun after all.

• • •

"Jenny!" The voice sounded far away. Jenny mumbled something and rolled over, but someone shook her shoulder. "Jenny, wake up! It's dinnertime."

Dinnertime? Jenny squinted up to see the Barbie doll leaning over her. What was her name? Sharon something. Her roommate.

"What?" Jenny croaked. She cleared her throat and tried again. "What do you mean, dinnertime? Don't you mean breakfast?"

Sharon laughed. "No, I mean dinner. It's five o'clock. You slept all day. We were beginning to wonder if you were dead."

Five o'clock! Jenny sat up quickly, holding both sides of her head. Her mouth tasted nasty, and her throat was dry. "Okay. Just give me a minute to get dressed. I guess I was more tired than I thought."

She quickly pulled on some shorts and a tee shirt. How on earth had she slept until five o'clock? She and Dean had planned to fix up the children's playroom today. He was probably wondering what had happened to her.

Dinner was a lot more fun this time. Jenny talked and joked with Sharon and met some of the other staff members. She felt like part of the group this time instead of a stupid little kid. She didn't even shriek when she saw a cockroach. By the time the passengers arrived, she would be a pro.

Her next few days were busy. She learned her way around the ship and worked on the playroom with Dean.

Her first glimpse of the small, narrow room was a little depressing. It was a mess, with boxes and other junk stacked everywhere. But once she and Dean started opening the boxes of toys, the job became a lot more fun.

"Hey, look at this!" Jenny said, pulling out a cardboard tube of Pickup Stix. "I haven't played with these since I was a kid!"

"Me neither," Dean said. "Want to play?"

"Sure!" Jenny shook the tube, then dumped the brightly colored sticks. "You go first."

Sitting cross-legged on the floor, they took turns lifting one stick at a time from the pile, trying not to jiggle any of the others. Jenny won the first game. They kept playing until Dean finally won a game.

"Well, I guess we'd better get back to work," he said, stretching. "This place is really a mess."

They found some board games in a box, but the instructions were all in Italian. Jenny opened one game that had a bunch of cards with little people heads on them. It looked like some kind of "matching game." They might have to make up their own instructions for all of the games if none of the kids spoke Italian.

Jenny's excitement grew as the day grew closer for the ship to leave. The paint cans and sheets of plastic disappeared from the ship's decks, and the crew polished all the glass and metal until it shone. The *Achille Lauro* was now one of the most beautiful ocean liners in the harbor. Jenny was proud to be one of the Starlight hostesses.

The day before the passengers were to arrive,

the captain ordered a lifeboat drill. Jenny was assigned to a lifeboat station, the place she would go to help passengers if a real emergency happened. Her practice station was in the Arazzi Lounge. The captain announced that the lifeboat drill would take place at two o'clock that afternoon.

At two o'clock sharp, the ship's horn sounded two long, mournful blasts: *Whaaa-aa-aaah! Whaaa-aa-aaah!* Even though she had been expecting it, the sound sent shivers down Jenny's spine. Somehow, until that moment, it had never occurred to her that the *Achille Lauro* could possibly sink. She dragged her life jacket out from under the bed in her cabin, then ran toward the lounge. To pass the drill, she had to get to her station quickly.

Several other Starlight staff members beat her to the station. Once they were all there, a safety officer came by to show them how to load the passengers onto lifeboats.

"If we have to abandon ship, women and children will be loaded first, forty to each lifeboat," he explained. "Then we load the rest of the passengers. Once all passengers are safe, the Starlight staff and the ship's crew will abandon ship. It's your job to make sure the passengers stay calm and get to the lifeboats."

Jenny swallowed, her mouth suddenly dry. The way he was talking made the whole thing sound so *real*!

"In the event of an emergency," the man went on, "the captain will send out a distress signal.

Every vessel that hears it is required by law to come to our aid."

By the time the man finished talking, Jenny's eyes were wide. She'd been a little nervous about flying to Italy, but she had never even thought about the ship sinking. Now, standing on deck watching the bright orange lifeboats being lowered, it seemed possible. Look at what had happened to the *Titanic*!

Jenny shook herself. Something like that could never happen. Not on the big, beautiful *Achille Lauro*!

The deep blast of the *Achille Lauro*'s horn quivered in the air. The hundreds of passengers lining the rails cheered. Waving at the people on the docks below, they began to throw the colorful streamers that Jenny and the other staff members had given them. They were on their way!

Jenny was standing by the rail along one of the upper decks, throwing paper streamers like everyone else. She waved at the crowd down on the docks, not caring that they were all strangers. Her heart pounded with excitement. This was it!

As the huge ship slowly backed away from the docks, Jenny stayed glued to the rail, not wanting to miss anything. She forgot for a moment that she worked there, even though she was wearing the Starlight uniform. She couldn't take her eyes off the water churning far below. It was strange, after living on the ship for a whole week, to feel it actually *move*!

Finally, she turned away with a sigh. The parents on board would soon come to the playroom to meet her and Dean. She had only spotted two or three children so far among the passengers. That was a relief. Now that the time had come to start her job, she was nervous. What if the kids didn't like her? What if their *parents* didn't like her? She had heard that several "V.I.P.s" (Very Important People) were on this cruise. She was glad Dean would be there.

Meeting the families wasn't so bad. One of the V.I.P.s—a French diplomat—had two girls, an eleven-year-old named Runel and her younger sister, Inelda. They both smiled shyly as their parents introduced them.

"Hello," Jenny said, patting them gingerly on their shoulders. They seemed to like it. Jenny breathed a silent sigh of relief. This baby-sitting thing might be easier than she'd thought.

An Italian couple brought in their two young sons, Alex and Andrew. After the family left, Jenny murmured to Dean, "Do you think Andrew's old enough to read? Maybe he can help us figure out all those Italian board games."

"He looks like he's only six or seven. I wouldn't count on it."

A single mother with a thick German or Dutch accent brought her four-year-old son to meet them. "This is Ruttgah," she said proudly. "Say hello, Ruttgah."

The boy hid behind his mother, peering out at them warily. He was short and stocky, with blond hair and blue eyes. Dean grinned and squatted down.

"We've got some great toys to play with," he said. "You want to see them?"

Ruttgah hesitated, then slowly edged out from behind his mother. Soon he was happily digging through one of the toy boxes with Dean.

Jenny met two blond sisters named Jean and Kim, then a three-year-old named Michael. Watching him rocket back and forth across the playroom, Jenny decided she'd leave him to Dean. He looked like a little devil!

Late that night, lying in her bunk, Jenny went back over the eight children she had met. They had all seemed quite nice, even the "Little Devil"—what was his name?—Michael.

I guess I'll find out tomorrow how nice they really are, she thought drowsily. Sharon was already asleep in her bunk across the small cabin, her Barbie-face buried in her pillow. Jenny imagined that by the time the *Achille Lauro* returned to Genoa, they would both be more than ready for a break.

At nine o'clock the next morning, Jenny met Dean in the playroom, ready to greet the children as they arrived for the day. Jenny had chosen a uniform with shorts instead of a skirt. She had a feeling she'd be spending a lot of time crawling around on the floor.

By eleven o'clock, most of the kids had been dropped off. By noon, the playroom was in chaos. Little Michael was fighting with Ruttgah over a ball. Alex and Andrew were fighting over some Legos. Runel, the oldest girl there, was already bored. None of them could read Italian, so the board games were useless.

"I took the wrong job," Jenny told Dean during a lull. She had just pulled Michael away from Ruttgah for the third time. "I don't know anything about kids. I'm no good at this."

Dean laughed. "You're doing fine. It's just the first day. They'll settle down."

"I'll bet," Jenny said darkly. It wasn't even lunchtime yet, and her uniform was already rumpled, her ponytail drooping. She felt like *she* needed a baby-sitter. She wished her mother was on board.

She turned back to the children, forcing a smile. "I have an idea," she said. "Why don't you each make a pretty drawing to hang on the wall?" To her surprise, the kids calmed right down. She passed out drawing paper and crayons, then watched as they all began to color. Even the Little Devil was hard at work.

Dean patted her on the back. "See? I told you you'd be a great baby-sitter. The secret is to keep them busy."

Jenny nodded, pleased with herself. When they weren't fighting, the kids weren't so bad. She was still

ABOVE: Jenny in playroom.

having trouble with a few of their names, but she was getting to know most of them. Some were shy, some were mischievous, and some were just plain hyper. Like the Little Devil . . .

As if reading her thoughts, Michael glanced up to give her an angelic smile, his chubby fingers still curled tightly around a green crayon. Jenny laughed, then straightened her ponytail with a firm tug. If she didn't watch out, she might end up falling in love with some of the little rascals.

The second night out, the captain threw a big party for all the passengers. Everybody dressed up for it. As Jenny and Sharon got ready, they checked out the "formal" uniforms they'd been given.

"Look at these poofy sleeves!" Jenny said, holding up the uniform dress. "They look like water wings. If I fell overboard in this thing, I'd just float."

Sharon laughed. "You look like a puffy penguin. I brought my own dress to wear tonight. Did you bring anything else to wear?"

"My grad dress. I love it, and I've only worn it once."

They chatted happily as they got ready. Jenny was still disgusted by her roommate's Barbie-like beauty, but Sharon wasn't at all vain. Jenny liked her a lot.

At the party, Jenny couldn't help staring at some of the women passengers. They were covered with diamonds and emeralds and gold. Most of them were older people with a lot of money. It made her graduation party seem like a kiddie party.

She wandered around for a while, then went out on deck to lean on the railing. The *Achille Lauro* was lit up like a Christmas tree, but the ocean all around looked black. It didn't feel like the ship was moving, but she knew it was. Far below, the black water churned as they sliced through it.

I'm out in the middle of the ocean on my way to Israel and Egypt, she told herself. *This is so cool. I can't wait to tell Mom and Juline about it when I get back.*

They reached Israel three days later. By then, Jenny had become a baby-sitting pro. The kids now ran up and hugged her whenever they saw her. Runel and Inelda, the French diplomat's daughters, told her stories about their life in France. Jenny learned that a pacifier soothed Michael when he was fussy, and that little Ruttgah loved to be helpful. She caught him out on deck once picking up wet towels for the old ladies. What a sweetheart!

"For someone who doesn't know anything about kids, you're doing a good job," Dean teased. "In fact, you're getting positively *motherly*!"

Jenny laughed. "I don't know about motherly, but I have to admit I'm getting a little attached to them. I'm probably going to cry when they all leave."

"Oh, great . . . that'll make them *all* start crying!" He shook his head. "But listen, can you do

me a favor? I've never been to Israel before, and
I'd like to go ashore and look around while we're
here. If you'll watch the kids by yourself this
time, I'll take over for you when we get to Egypt."

"Are we allowed to do that?"

"Sure! Most of the kids go ashore with their
parents. You'll only have one or two."

As soon as the *Achille Lauro* docked, the ship
emptied. Jenny was a little sad that she couldn't
go ashore, but she comforted herself with the
thought that Egypt was only one day's travel
away. It sounded so mysterious. Pyramids, the
Sphinx . . . all the things she'd read about in
school, she'd now see with her own eyes!

Only the two youngest children, Alex and Michael, stayed on board. Jenny took them swim-
ming in the pool, then let them play their own
version of shuffleboard out on deck. The ship was
practically deserted.

It was late that afternoon when the passengers
came streaming back on board like ants. Dean
showed up with a sunburn and a tacky stool. It
had a bunch of little camels carved into its legs.

"Ve-ry nice," Jenny said skeptically when he
showed it to her. "What are you going to do with
it?"

Dean glared at her. "I don't know. Sit on it, I
guess. I just thought it looked interesting."

"Uh-huh. Couldn't you find any *non*-tacky sou-
venirs?" She jumped away, laughing, as Dean
tried to poke her with his stool.

Runel and Inelda soon ran up, bubbling over
with news about their day in Israel.

"I wish you could've come, Jenny," Runel said, bouncing up and down. "It was great. We walked right where Jesus walked, on the very same ground. And we saw the place where he was buried!"

"*And*—" Inelda interrupted, "we got these papers that said we were Official Pilgrims! I got one and Runel got one."

Jenny smiled. "Sounds great. I wish I could've come, but I had to baby-sit Michael and Alex. I'll be going ashore in Egypt, though."

"Good!" Runel said. "Maybe you can come with us!"

The *Achille Lauro* left port a few hours later. As they cruised through the dark seas toward Egypt, Jenny slept peacefully, dreaming of pyramids against a sunny sky.

"Lady! Camel ride, very cheap. You come?"

Jenny shook her head and tried to walk faster. The tour director on the ship had warned her that the "camel drivers" often robbed people. Besides, the camels smelled bad.

"Lady!" The man wouldn't give up. He trotted along after her. "We take your picture, only five dollars!"

"No, thanks," Jenny said. But like lightning, the man grabbed her camera from her hands. He stepped back, still smiling, as a second man wrapped a colorful scarf around Jenny's head. The first man quickly snapped her picture.

"Five dollars, please." He held out his hand. Jenny glared at him, but if she wanted her camera back, it looked like she'd have to pay him. She handed him the money.

She was in Cairo, the capital of Egypt. On the bus ride from the ship, she had seen the Great Sphinx and three pyramids. They were all much bigger than she'd expected. The pyramids looked like mountains made from giant bricks. She had also seen the famous Nile River.

Now, exploring the city, she felt almost over-whelmed. The streets were narrow and winding, lined with booths where robe-clad people shouted at her, trying to get her to buy their clay pots and scarves. If she didn't watch out, she'd end up with something even tackier than Dean's camel stool!

She was looking for the City of the Dead, a huge cemetery everybody said she should see. When she found it, she was surprised. It didn't look like a cemetery. There were tiny houses built on top of all the graves—with people living in them!

"Long ago," explained the Arab tour guide, "families built houses on top of graves so they could mourn their loved ones in peace. Later, some moved into the houses. Today many fami-lies live in the City of the Dead."

How weird, Jenny thought, watching a little boy playing outside one of the houses. *I wouldn't want to live on top of somebody's grave!*

By the time she got back to the ship, she was hot, tired, and dusty. She went straight to her cabin to clean up. She smiled as she twisted the old-fashioned "hot" and "cold" shower knobs, try-ing to get the water just the right temperature.

This crazy old *Titanic* shower, she thought fondly. It might be ugly, but at least it worked . . . unlike the real *Titanic*'s showers, which must be scattered somewhere on the bottom of the ocean.

Jenny frowned. That wasn't a good thing to think about while she was miles out at sea. She pushed the thought away.

After leaving Egypt, the *Achille Lauro* wasn't due to reach the next port for six days. The passengers settled into daily routines that kept Jenny, Dean, and Sharon all busy.

Their third day at sea was Dean's twenty-first birthday. Jenny helped plan a surprise birthday party for him at dinner that night. The chef baked a birthday cake, and the staff chipped in to buy Dean a watch and some cologne. He had a great time.

Late that night, after finishing their work, Jenny and Sharon went to the Disco to get a snack. They were talking quietly when a crew member ran in and looked around. He ran over to a group of ship's officers and said something. Instantly, they all jumped up and rushed out.

Jenny turned to Sharon in alarm. "What's going on?"

"Must be a fight or something," Sharon said. "Let's go see!"

They followed the men outside. As they stepped out on deck, they could see huge sparks shooting out from somewhere above them. The sparks were falling like fireworks into the water all around them.

They both froze, unable to believe their eyes. They were still staring when the ship's deep horn suddenly shattered the night: *Whaa-aa-aah . . . Whaa-aa-aah!*

It was the emergency signal. The ship was on fire!

"Hurry, Jenny!" Sharon panted.

Racing downstairs toward their cabin, Jenny and Sharon took three steps at a time. They had to get their life jackets before they could go to their stations. All over the ship, cabin doors were popping open. Passengers ran out, then looked around in sleepy confusion. Most were in their nightgowns and pajamas.

"Go to your stations!" Sharon shouted to them. "Get your life jackets and go to your stations!"

Reaching their own cabin, Jenny and Sharon snatched up their life jackets. A faint smoky smell was drifting down the hallway now. Jenny felt like she was in some kind of bad dream. This couldn't be happening!

Jenny and Sharon were assigned to the same station in the Scarabeo Lounge. When they arrived, there were only a few passengers and other staff members waiting. The passengers all looked scared and upset.

"Hi!" Jenny said breathlessly. "My name's Jenny. Is everybody okay?"

"What's going on?" demanded one woman. She

was very large, dressed in a short, neon pink nightgown. She looked mad.

"I'm not sure," Jenny answered truthfully. "I think there's a fire somewhere."

As more passengers showed up, Jenny checked to make sure they had their life jackets. If not, she sent them back to their cabins to get them. At both ends of the lounge, the automatic fire doors started slamming shut. The sound made all of them jump.

They had only been in the Scarabeo Lounge for about ten minutes when the lights went out. Jenny gasped. The emergency lights immediately came on, but they were very dim. In the near-darkness, one woman started shrieking.

"We're going to die!" she said hysterically. "We're all going to die!" Jenny ran over and tried to calm her down. She was upsetting the other passengers. That was all they needed!

Suddenly, the intercom crackled. *"Attention, passengers!"* a deep voice boomed. *"The captain has asked that everyone move out onto the deck now. Repeat, everybody out onto the deck."* The instructions were repeated in Italian, French, and Dutch.

"Okay, everyone move this way," directed a staff member near the stairs. "We have to go upstairs."

Jenny and Sharon helped herd the passengers toward the stairs. Sharon went ahead to help the passengers out on deck, while Jenny stayed behind to make sure everybody got out of the lounge. When she got up on deck, Jenny spotted

Sharon and waved. It was nice to know that her roommate was nearby.

The ocean air was chilly. Some of the elderly passengers started to shiver. Jenny, afraid they'd get sick, volunteered to go back into the ship with some other staff members to find blankets. Sharon said she would come along, too.

Together, they started back down into the ship. The smoke was much worse now. Eyes burning, Jenny and Sharon bundled up as many blankets as they could find. By the time they got back out on deck, they were both coughing.

"Here, ma'am," Jenny said, draping a blanket across the shoulders of a frail elderly woman. A man wearing flannel pajamas with little puppy dogs all over them said he was okay, so she kept going. Soon most of the passengers had blankets.

One older lady smiled at Jenny. "I can't believe a little girl like you is taking care of us. You should get a blanket and go sit down. We should all be taking care of you!"

Jenny smiled back. "Thanks, but this is my job. I'm okay. I've been running around too much to get cold!"

For the next several hours, Jenny and Sharon walked up and down the deck, talking and joking with the passengers. They were trying to keep their spirits up. Most of the passengers were tired and scared. It was hard to ignore the torch-like sparks shooting up from the ship's main smokestack, or the smoke billowing out the sides. Wherever the fire was, it wasn't small.

Suddenly, Jenny heard a young voice shouting

her name. It was Runel. She ran over to hug Jenny, followed by Inelda. Both girls looked scared.

"What's going to happen?" Runel asked. "Is the ship going to sink?"

"Oh, I don't think so," Jenny said, stroking their dark hair. "I think they're just having a hard time putting out the fire."

"Can you stay here with us for a while?" Inelda asked. Jenny nodded and let herself be pulled over to a chair. The girls seemed to need her company.

She needed to find something to take their minds off what was going on. "So, Inelda," she said, "what's the first thing you're going to do when you get home?"

It worked. The scared look on the little girl's face disappeared. "I think I'll go over to my friend's house," she said, her face brightening. "She won't believe me when I tell her about this!"

"It's pretty exciting, isn't it? What about you, Runel?"

The older girl was harder to distract, but before long, Jenny had them both laughing. She finally stood up.

"Well, I need to go check on the other passengers. You girls stay out of trouble, okay?"

They both giggled. "Okay. Bye, Jenny!"

It was almost three o'clock in the morning. Jenny yawned. Why was it taking so long to put out a fire? She was making her way back toward the passengers she was in charge of when she saw a crowd gathering at one end of the ship. She broke into a run.

"What's going on?" she asked as she passed a crew member.

"A passenger's had a heart attack. The medical team is on its way."

Oh, great, Jenny thought. She slowed down, tempted to run the other way. But she could hear a woman crying, and the passengers were probably upset. She kept going.

By the time she made it through the crowd, the medical team had arrived. They were bending over an elderly man who was lying on the deck. He wasn't moving. Jenny quickly looked away. For the first time, she felt panicky. This was terrible!

"Okay, everyone get back!" she ordered. "Let's give them some room!" The passengers slowly obeyed, clearing the area. Jenny went with them.

A few minutes later, she heard that the man had died. She rubbed her forehead, wishing none of this were real. But she had passengers to care for. She couldn't curl up in a blanket and hide, no matter how bad she felt.

It was almost a relief to hear a familiar fussy wail. It was the Little Devil. She followed the sound until she found him. His mother was holding him, but he wouldn't stop crying. Jenny patted his back, knowing what he wanted.

"Do you have his pacifier?" she asked. "That usually calms him down when he's like this."

His mother shook her head tiredly. "We left it

in the cabin, and they won't let us go back in to get it."

Jenny bit her lip. "We have one in the play-room. I'll see if I can get it for you."

Just then she spotted Dean. She waved him over and explained. Dean volunteered to go with her to get the pacifier.

The trip into the burning ship was much worse this time. The smoke was thicker, and the metal walls were hot. Even though the playroom wasn't far from the deck, Jenny was relieved to emerge from the smoke again, pacifier in hand.

She popped it into Michael's mouth, cutting off the sound. He calmed down, munching on it happily. Soon he was asleep on his mother's shoulder.

The next several hours passed slowly. Passengers huddled in deck chairs and slept, or talked quietly in small groups. Jenny paced back and forth, watching the sparks and smoke blowing out over the dark waves.

It was only gradually that she noticed that the deck beneath her feet was starting to tilt. One by one, the passengers began to notice the same thing.

"Why is the ship tilting so much?" one woman asked, holding onto her husband's arm. "Are we sinking?"

"I don't know, ma'am. I don't think so. If we were sinking, they'd make us abandon ship. Try not to worry."

Easy enough to tell *them* that, Jenny thought

as she walked away. The trouble was, she was starting to wonder the same thing!

The sun slowly came up. The dazed and sleepy passengers looked worse in daylight. So did the *Achille Lauro*. The darkness had hidden most of the thick black smoke belching from the side of the ship. Now they could see it clearly, as it was carried away by the wind.

Jenny held onto the railing, trying to stay calm. This was getting bad. The deck was now tilted so far to port—the left side of the ship— that it was hard to stand up. If it got any worse, they would *have* to abandon ship!

"We're going to die, aren't we?"

Jenny jumped. The question had come from a woman passenger standing a few feet away. She sounded very matter-of-fact.

"No, ma'am," Jenny said firmly. She pushed away her own doubts. "This is a good, sturdy ship. And if we have to abandon it, we have plenty of lifeboats. We'll be okay."

The woman, comforted, walked away. Jenny stayed at the rail. The sea was rough, crashing against the sides of the ship. The lifeboats would be tossed around like toy boats if they had to use them. And with the ship leaning over so far, she wasn't sure the lifeboats on the higher side could even be launched. There might not be enough lifeboats for everybody.

The intercom crackled. Jenny froze, waiting for the announcement she suddenly realized she was dreading.

"Attention, passengers. The captain has issued the order to abandon ship. We will start loading lifeboats from the port side, women and children first. Please stay calm and obey instructions from the crew."

It was really happening. The *Achille Lauro* was going down!

"Be careful going down the stairs, ma'am. That's right, take it slow." Jenny kept a firm grip on the elderly woman's arm until she saw that she was holding onto the rail.

The first lifeboat filled up fast. Jenny and Sharon stood on the deck above the loading area, helping guide the passengers to the stairs. Dean was just below, helping load the women and children into the boats. Jenny's eyes were stinging from the smoke in the air.

She looked around frantically, trying to find all the children. She wanted to make sure they made it onto the lifeboats. She was relieved to spot Runel and Inelda heading her way. They were clinging to their mom and dad. Inelda was sobbing.

"Hi, girls!" Jenny said, waving. "Over here!"

When they reached her, Jenny gave them each a big hug. "Listen to me," she said in her sternest "playroom" voice. "Dean's waiting down there to put you into a nice big lifeboat. You just need to be strong and stay calm so you don't scare your mother. Okay?"

The girls nodded. They didn't want to scare their mom. "Are you coming, Jenny?" Runel asked.

"We have to get all the passengers off the ship first, but I'll be coming pretty soon." She smiled and pushed them toward the stairs. "Now go on. I'll see you on the next ship!"

Michael and his parents eventually showed up, but Jenny never saw Ruttgah or the others. She stared out at the lifeboats bobbing in the waves, but as soon as they were loaded, they moved away from the ship. She couldn't make out any faces.

They slowly made their way around the ship, lowering the lifeboats that were strapped along the sides. They also used some inflatable lifeboats. To reach the inflatable boats, passengers had to climb down flimsy rope ladders. Jenny and Sharon held their breath as several elderly passengers edged their way down the ladders. What would happen if they fell? The waves would smash them against the ship!

When the crew started loading the men passengers, Jenny shoved her way over to Dean. "Did all the kids make it into lifeboats? I saw Runel, Inelda, and Michael, but I didn't see any of the others!"

Dean nodded. "I saw all eight of them. I made sure they got on lifeboats."

"Oh, good." Her mind relieved, Jenny went back to helping the passengers. Lifeboat by lifeboat, they worked their way around to the high side of the ship. The boats on that side were much harder to lower. Instead of falling straight down into the water, they hit the side of the tilted ship. One wouldn't lower at all.

"Do you think we're going to run out of life-boats?" Jenny asked Sharon in a low voice. "We're down to just four. And look at how many passengers are left!"

Sharon looked pale. "I know. This isn't good."

Toward the middle of the ship, the air grew hotter, the smoke thicker. The *Achille Lauro* was fully ablaze now, with flames shooting out from the upper decks. They were down to their next-to-last lifeboat.

Jenny glanced at the line of men passengers still waiting. Each boat held forty people. Fear knotted her stomach. What if there wasn't a boat left for the Starlight staff and the crew? Would they just have to swim, hoping their life jackets would hold them up until a rescue ship came?

"Jenny, look at this."

Sharon pointed to the metal wall right behind them. Jenny stared, horrified. The gray paint was *bubbling* from the heat, sizzling and popping like frying eggs. As she watched, the paint slowly turned a black, charred color.

"We've got to get off this ship," Jenny said, breathing fast. "This is crazy. What if it explodes or something?"

"Yeah, well, just don't lean on the wall," Sharon said weakly, trying to make a joke. "It might be a little warm."

Finally, the last passenger was loaded. Dean motioned to Jenny and Sharon. "There's still some room left in this boat!" he called. "Come on!"

Other Starlight staff members quickly followed

them into the boat. The moment it was full, the crew began to lower it. It went down toward the water in sharp jerks, rocking and banging against the side of the ship. Jenny held on, terrified. This was almost worse than staying on the burning ship!

As soon as they hit the water, the crew member in charge started the motor and pointed the lifeboat away from the ship. Jenny twisted around to look back, unable to take her eyes off the *Achille Lauro*. The once beautiful ocean liner was sagging sideways in the water, filled with flames and belching oily smoke. Jenny pictured her cabin on board: the family snapshots she'd pinned on the wall curling up and burning . . . Juline's tiny glass Christmas tree shattering from the heat . . . her favorite gold locket, a gift from her grandmother, melting and turning black. Then all of it sinking down, down, into the darkness.

Tears filled her eyes. She wished she had never set foot on the *Achille Lauro*. It was too painful to watch it die.

The sound of vomiting jerked Jenny's attention back from the ship. Several passengers were leaning over the sides, sickened by the up-and-down movement of the lifeboat. She was almost glad for the distraction. It reminded her that she had a job to do. Her gloomy thoughts would just have to wait.

They kept going until the *Achille Lauro* looked

like a toy ship in the distance. When they spotted several other lifeboats, they formed a "chain" by tying ropes from boat to boat. It was better to stay together while they waited for rescue.

"How long do you think it'll be before a ship comes to pick us up?" Jenny asked Sharon. The tropical sun already felt like a furnace. "I'm afraid for some of these guys. They're not in very good shape."

"It shouldn't be too long. There are lots of ships out here, and they're supposed to drop everything and come running in an emergency."

They did their best to comfort the passengers, passing out cups of water and encouraging them. But one hour passed, then two, with no sign of rescue. Jenny, sweaty and sunburned, began to get discouraged. What was taking so long?

Then someone on one of the other boats shouted, "Look!"

A weak cheer went up as they all saw the ship in the distance. It was heading straight for them!

Sharon leaned over to hug Jenny. Her perfect Barbie nose was burned bright red by the sun, and her blond Barbie hair was sticky with sweat. "I guess we're not going to die after all," she said.

Jenny grinned. "I guess not." They both laughed, then turned to watch the approaching ship.

The *Hawaiian King* was a Greek oil tanker. As it got closer, Jenny could see tiny stick-figure people on the deck, waving. It wasn't until the *Hawaiian King* stopped a short distance from them that the stick figures turned into Greek sailors. They waved at the lifeboats.

Jenny joined the sunburned passengers in waving back and yelling, "Over here!" They were all anxious to get out of the lifeboats.

The seas were too rough for the *Hawaiian King* to lower its gangplank. The *Achille Lauro* passengers would have to climb rope ladders to get onto the ship. It would be a long, hard climb.

Jenny and Sharon held their breath as the passengers from another lifeboat inched up the swinging rope ladder. After bobbing around for hours in the rolling waves, many of the elderly passengers were sunburned and seasick. What if they couldn't make the long climb?

Everyone from the first lifeboat made it up safely. Now it was their turn.

Jenny and Sharon hung back with the other Starlight staff members to let the passengers go first. While she waited, Jenny tried to find the lifeboats carrying the children. She wished they could have been picked up first.

Finally, it was her turn. "See you up on deck!" she told Sharon. The ladder jerked back and forth as she climbed, almost flinging her off. She gritted her teeth and held on tight, glad she had on a life jacket.

Two Greek sailors helped her up the last few feet. Jenny laughed with relief when her feet finally hit the nice, solid deck of the *Hawaiian King*. It felt great to be on a ship again, and one that wasn't burning or sinking!

Jenny looked around to make sure the passengers were all okay. Since nobody seemed to need her, she decided to stay close to the ladder and watch for the children. They would probably be scared after everything that had happened.

Ruttgah and his mother were on the fourth or fifth lifeboat. The little boy started scrambling up the ladder like a monkey, but his mother couldn't follow. She was a big woman, and she couldn't pull herself up onto the rope ladder. Ruttgah stopped after a few feet.

"Come on, Mommy!" he called.

His mother tried again, but she still couldn't get onto the ladder. "You go ahead with somebody else, honey," she said. "Mommy will be there in a few minutes."

Jenny, watching from above, called down, "Come on, Ruttgah! You can wait up here with me!"

The little boy's face lit up when he saw her. "Jenny!" he squealed. With another passenger close behind, he climbed the rest of the way up to the ship.

Jenny swept him up in a bear hug. "Ruttgah! I'm so happy to see you. Are you okay?"

"Yes. But my mommy can't climb the ladder." As usual, Ruttgah was more concerned about others than about himself.

"They'll find a way to get her up here," Jenny assured him. "Why don't you come sit with me back here, away from the edge? I don't want you falling in."

She sat down on a big pipe and pulled Ruttgah

onto her lap. She tried to distract him as the Greek sailors lowered a sling—sort of like a hammock—for his mother. The sling swung wildly as they pulled her up, but she made it safely onto deck.

Returning Ruttgah to his mother, Jenny went back to watch for the other children. When Michael showed up, Jenny smiled and hugged him. He might be the Little Devil, but she was happy to see him.

One by one, all eight kids climbed onto the *Hawaiian King*. Runel and Inelda were relieved to find Jenny waiting for them at the top of the ladder. They both grabbed her.

"We did what you said," Runel told her. "We stayed calm so Mom wouldn't get scared."

"Good for you! I'm proud of both of you. And now you'll have even more to tell your friends when you get home, right?"

"Yeah!" When the girls walked off with their parents, they were both smiling.

It was almost funny when Jean and Kim, the blond sisters, showed up a few minutes later. Their mother really *was* scared, and they were trying their best to calm her down.

"It's okay, Mom. We're safe now," Jean said. Her mother was trembling and sobbing. In a whisper, Kim explained to Jenny that their mother was afraid of water. She had cried almost the whole time they were in the lifeboat.

Jenny hugged the girls, even though they didn't seem to need comforting. "You're doing a good job," she whispered back. "She'll probably calm down now that we're back on a real ship."

"I hope so," Kim said.

Jenny didn't relax until the last child had boarded the *Hawaiian King*. Then she leaned against the rail, almost too tired to stand up. It had been over forty hours since she had slept. Now that she knew all the kids were safe, she felt like collapsing.

In the distance, tall flames were still leaping into the sky from the *Achille Lauro*. Jenny shuddered and turned away. She didn't want to watch the dying ship disappear beneath the waves. She didn't want to remember the smell of smoke, or the blistering paint. She didn't want to think about all her possessions that would disappear forever with the ship.

Tears stung her eyes. Now that the crisis was over, she didn't feel like a grown-up Starlight staff member any more. She just felt like a tired, frightened seventeen-year-old who wanted her mother.

"Mom?" Jenny pressed the radio phone to her ear, trying to hear the faint voice on the other end. "Mom? It's me, Jenny!"

"Jenny!" Her mother's happy shriek came through loud and clear this time. "Honey, where are you? Are you okay?"

It had been three days since the *Hawaiian King* had picked up the *Achille Lauro* castaways. On the second day, they had all been transferred to another Greek ship, the *Chios*. The Communications Officer had kindly offered to let Jenny use the expensive ship-to-shore radio to call home.

Now, hearing her mother's voice, Jenny felt her throat grow tight. She *couldn't* start crying—not when the call was costing the ship forty dollars per minute!

"I'm okay, Mom," she managed to choke out. "I just wanted to let you know I'm alive and everything. I'll be in Kenya in two days, and I'll call you again from there."

"Jenny, don't you hang up!" Her mom sounded hysterical. "Where are you? We've been calling everywhere, trying to find out if you were okay!"

"I'm on a Greek ship called the *Chios*. But I really can't talk now. I just wanted to say—" Jenny broke off, swallowed, and tried again: "I just wanted to say I love you."

"Oh, Jen, I love you too. Call me again as soon as you can, okay?"

"I will. Bye, Mom."

As she handed the radiophone back to the officer, Jenny almost felt worse than she had before she called. She was glad that her mom knew she was okay, but now she felt like a homesick kid. Could she really handle this job for another six months? Maybe she should just quit and go back home.

Discouraged, she walked back out onto the deck. She didn't look up until someone called her name. Sharon was standing with a group of other

Starlight staff members who waved for her to join them.

Sharon moved over so Jenny could join their laughing group. "Did you get to talk to your mom?" she asked.

Jenny nodded miserably. "Yeah . . . it made me kind of homesick."

Taren, another staff member, gave her a sharp look. "Hey, you're not thinking about quitting on us, are you? We need you, Jenny. Especially after all we've been through!"

Sharon quickly agreed. "You've done a great job! And I was counting on having you as my roommate on our next cruise. Don't you dare quit!"

One by one, the others agreed. "You were wonderful with the kids." "You really kept the passengers calm." "We couldn't have done it without you!"

Jenny felt a weight slowly lifting from her shoulders. She might be feeling weak now, but when it really counted, she hadn't wimped out. Why should she start now?

She burst out laughing. "Okay!" she said. "You've convinced me that I'm wonderful. I'll stay. I just hope the next ship we're on doesn't sink or burn or explode."

"Of course, we might hit an iceberg," Sharon suggested helpfully. "Or maybe get torpedoed. Wouldn't that be exciting?"

"No!" Jenny said. "I'm ready for a nice, boring cruise. I've had enough adventure to last me for a long, long time."

Jenny Peterson's actions during the Achille Lauro *crisis earned her a silver medal for merit from the Royal Life Saving Society of Canada.*

This story was submitted by reader Maureen Goldman of Gibsons, B.C., Canada.

Boarding *Hawaiian King.*

A Deadly Gas!

THE JUSTIN HOCKLEY STORY

ABOVE: Tenderfoot Scout Justin Hockley.

"Oof!" Justin gasped as a big fist caught him squarely in the stomach. Dazed, the twelve-year-old swung wildly, but his fist hit empty air. The man was now behind him, jabbing at his back.

"Come on, Justin!" he prompted. "Elbows in and chin down. You're leaving yourself wide open!"

Norm, a boxing coach in Sturgis, South Dakota, was a tall man with graying hair, a wide smile, and huge fists. He trained a group of boys in the basement of the local Veterans of Foreign Wars (VFW) Club. They had built a homemade ring there that looked like the real thing.

"I'm trying!" Justin mumbled around his mouth guard. Norm made them all put on full headgear, boxing gloves, and plastic mouth guards before they got in the ring. Justin felt a spit string dribbling from the corner of his mouth and sucked it back in. Mouth guards were gross.

The other boys cheered him on as he ducked, jabbed, and swung at Norm, determined to land a few good punches. By the time the three-minute round ended, Justin was out of breath. He spat his mouth guard out into his glove and smacked his lips. He was always amazed at how tired he could get in three measly minutes!

Norm clubbed him warmly on the shoulder with his gloved hand. "Good job, Justin. You have a mean left hook. You got me there a few times!"

Justin grinned. "Thanks." He was left-handed, which gave him an advantage. Since this was only his fifth boxing lesson, he needed every advantage he could get. He still had a lot to learn.

After class the boys all walked outside together. "Hey, Justin, your mom's here," one boy called. "And she's driving the Ghostbuster!"

Justin grinned. The Ghostbuster was his mom's big, white 1970 Suburban. It used to be an ambulance. It still had a sliding glass divider behind the driver's seat, and a red "No Smoking" sign in the back. Somebody had bolted a seat in the back where the

RIGHT TO LEFT: Justin, Jess and Rachele.

injured people used to go. The Suburban was big and ugly, but it was *fast*. Justin loved it. It even had cabinets in the back where he could put all his stuff.

Jess and Rachele, Justin's younger brother and sister, both hated the Ghostbuster. They kept hoping it would break down and die, but it never did. That was why their mother liked it so much.

"She just keeps going," Mrs. Hockley often said, patting the Suburban's dashboard. "And she can carry an army!" Jess's suggestion that they *give* her to the army fell on deaf ears.

Mrs. Hockley smiled and waved when she saw Justin. She looked relieved. She hated boxing, and was always afraid he was going to get his brains bashed out.

Justin climbed into the front seat beside her. "Hi, mom. Here I am, still alive. No brains oozing out anywhere, even. See?" He twisted his head around so she could check out both sides.

Louise Hockley mumbled, "No brains inside, either." She jammed the Ghostbuster into reverse. "I still don't know why you want to come here and let people hit you."

Justin gave her a pitying glance. "It's a guy thing, Mom. It's hand-to-hand combat. You wouldn't understand."

Mrs. Hockley sighed. She was tall with light brown hair and foofy bangs. She worked as a nurse's aide and sometimes as a lunch lady at a local school. She was an okay mom, except for her attitude about boxing.

Jess and Mr. Hockley were watching TV when

they got home. Rachele, as usual, was playing with all her Barbies and trolls. She was only eight, and she squealed if anybody stepped on her dolls. Since she spread them all over the floor, it was like walking through a mine field to get past her.

"Hi," Justin said to anybody who was listening. "I'm home!"

Del Hockley smiled. "Hi, son. How was boxing practice?"

With a loud sigh, Mrs. Hockley stalked off into the kitchen. Justin grinned. "It was great, Dad. I fought Norm today. He beat me pretty bad, but he said I had a mean left hook!"

"Good for you!" Mr. Hockley was a Vietnam veteran who served now in the National Guard. *He* thought boxing was great. If he hadn't insisted that it was good exercise for Justin, Mrs. Hockley would never have allowed him to go. Justin was a little pudgy, so she was always looking for ways to get him to exercise. Justin had never figured out why she wanted him to play football, where he got bashed and run over, but hated boxing. Mothers! Who could figure them out?

On his way to take a quick shower before Boy Scouts, Justin pretended to step on one of Rachele's goofy Barbies. She snatched it up, squeaking, "Justin!" He liked making Rachele squeak. She sounded like a little mouse when you stepped on its tail. A freckled, squeaky little mouse-sister, that's what he had!

His brother, Jess, was a different story. He was ten, but he was tough. Back when Jess and Justin had still shared a room, their mom had put a strip of masking tape down the middle of the floor to keep them from fighting. Jess was a neat freak, so his half of the room always looked clean. Justin sometimes threw his stuff over on Jess's side just to aggravate him.

Wednesday nights were always crazy around their house, especially now that Justin had started boxing. He went straight from school to boxing, stayed there until five o'clock, then raced home and got ready for Boy Scouts. Scouts lasted from six till seven, then he went straight to church for Wednesday night Youth Group. By the time he finally got home to stay, he was exhausted.

"Justin!" his mom called. "You'd better hurry up and shower, or you'll be late for Scouts."

"I'm going, I'm going," he grumbled.

As usual, he barely made it to Boy Scouts in time. He was a Tenderfoot, but his uniform was dirty and he hadn't had time to wash it. He showed up in "civilian" clothes for a change.

The Boy Scouts met each week in a small gym in town. When Justin walked in, the older boys were all racing around shooting hoops. Mr. Jones, the Scout Master, sat at a table chatting with the younger scouts. He was an older man, tall and skinny with gray hair combed straight back. He had probably trained hundreds of Boy Scouts.

Finally, Mr. Jones called the meeting to order. One boy read the minutes from their last meeting, then they talked about a fund-raiser they were planning. Once all the boring stuff was out of the way, it was time to work on their merit badges.

The boys split into two groups for that. Ken, the Assistant Scout Master, took the younger Scouts off to one side of the room; Mr. Jones and the older Scouts sat at the table. The older boys were working on their Safety Merit Badge now.

Mr. Jones cleared his throat. "We're going to go over some information tonight about different hazards you should watch for around the house. But first, did any of you bring back your safety checklists?"

A couple of hands went up, including Justin's. Several weeks before, Mr. Jones had passed out a home inspection checklist. To fulfill that requirement for the Safety Merit Badge, each boy had to make an inspection of their home and explain the different hazards they found.

"Good!" said Mr. Jones. "Let's hear what you came up with."

One boy had found a frayed extension cord that could possibly start a fire. He had convinced his mom to replace it with a new one. Another boy had discovered that one of their smoke alarms had a dead battery. Several mentioned furnaces and fireplaces as possible fire hazards.

Mr. Jones nodded in approval. "That's good. With fireplaces and furnaces, though, fires and explosions aren't the only things you have to watch for. How many of you have heard of carbon monoxide poisoning?"

Most of them nodded. "Good," Mr. Jones said. "Carbon monoxide is an invisible, odorless, tasteless gas that kills a lot of people each year. You've probably heard that fireplaces and furnaces can produce it. But did you know that cars, outdoor grills, and dryers can, too, if they're broken or not ventilated properly?"

He quickly went over the early symptoms of carbon monoxide poisoning: headaches, nausea, drowsiness, and flu-like symptoms. "Eventually," he concluded, "it sends people into a dead sleep—literally! They lose consciousness and won't wake up. That's why you shouldn't mess around if a chimney becomes blocked, or if a dryer or gas stove starts to malfunction. Call a repairman and get it fixed."

Justin nodded, doodling on a paper in front of him. He was tempted to skip church tonight, but they were going to be talking about teen suicide. It sounded interesting. Terry, their pastor, was a big, jolly man with a deep voice. He and Don Ericsson, a member of the local fire department, took turns leading the Youth Group.

Distracted, Justin barely listened to the rest of the safety discussion. He already knew most of the stuff. After all, his mom was a nurse.

"Hey, Justin, wait up!"

Justin paused in the hallway at Sturgis Williams Middle School to let his friend Josh catch up. Josh lived on a ranch nearby, and the two boys often got together after school or on weekends to go hiking. The Black Hills were right next to Justin's house.

Justin asked, "What's up?"

Josh was a couple of inches taller than Justin. He kept his hair buzzed short on both sides. "I wanted to see what you were doing this weekend. You feel like doing something tomorrow?"

Justin shrugged. "Maybe. We could hike up and see if that fort we built is still there. You know, the one we made with that big limestone rock."

"I know the *rock's* still there," Josh said. "It would take a giant to move it. Just call me later, okay?"

"Sure."

Shuffling down the hall toward Mr. Shuck's math class, Justin smiled. The last time he and Josh had gone camping, they had found a rock cave made out of a limestone boulder. They built a shelter out of it by leaning branches against the opening. That night, they had cleared a small area in front and built a fire. It had been a lot of fun.

Since it was Friday, Justin didn't have boxing practice after school. He rode the school bus, then walked almost a mile from the bus stop to his house.

When he walked in the front door, he wrinkled his nose. There was that funny smell again! They'd had their propane furnace fixed several weeks before, and ever since then, there'd been a faint oily smell in the air. Mrs. Hockley had made the repairmen come back out to check the furnace again, but they said it was fine. Maybe the smell was stuck to their curtains and furniture. Justin hoped it wore off soon. It made him feel queasy.

"Mom!" he yelled. "I'm home!"

Mrs. Hockley appeared in the hallway. "Hi, honey. How was school?"

"It was alright. Josh and I are thinking about going hiking tomorrow up in the Black Hills." Justin caught another whiff of oily air and wrinkled his nose. "Listen, that smell in here is still really bad. I think you should call the furnace people again."

Mrs. Hockley looked surprised. She sniffed the air. "I don't smell anything."

"You're just used to it. Trust me, it stinks in here."

"Okay. I'll call them, but they keep saying there's nothing wrong. I wish they'd figure it out."

"Me too. Furnaces can blow up, you know. Kaboom! No more house, and no more us. Just little pieces everywhere."

Mrs. Hockley smiled. "Thanks, Justin. That makes me feel *much* better!"

That evening, Justin and Josh made plans to go hiking. They decided to sleep in the next morning and leave right after lunch. Neither of them liked the idea of waking up early on a Saturday.

It was chilly the next day, but the sky over the Black Hills was bright and clear. When Josh showed up, Justin grabbed his Boy Scout canteen and not much else. They only planned to be gone a few hours.

"So, how's boxing going?" Josh asked as they scrambled up the first small, rocky slope. Parts of the Black Hills were almost flat, but other parts were steep. There were a lot of trees.

"Fine," Justin said, puffing a little. "It's fun. You ought to start coming."

"Nah, I don't think so. I like football and stuff better."

Justin smiled. "Maybe we ought to trade moms. My mom *hates* boxing. She gets upset every time I go."

Josh laughed. "What does your dad say?"

"He says I need the exercise." Justin patted his well-rounded stomach with satisfaction. "I guess this is one time when being a little, uh, *big* comes in handy."

Something rustled in the bushes nearby. "Shh!" Josh said. "Let's go see what that is!"

They walked quietly, tiptoeing over broken branches and gravel. When they got close to the bushes, a small gray-brown shape darted out and scampered away.

"A chipmunk!" Justin said. "Haven't seen one of those in a while."

They wandered on, stopping now and then to look at an interesting rock or tree. Justin knew from Boy Scouts to be careful when poking around rock piles. Rattlesnakes often hid there, enjoying the sun. They buzzed angrily if you disturbed them . . . and if you were close enough, they struck. It wouldn't be much fun to get snake-bit miles from home.

The boys had just stepped out of the trees when they saw movement in a clearing just ahead. A flock of about twenty wild turkeys were milling around, pecking at bugs and seeds in the grass. They were big, stupid-looking birds with little heads.

Justin and Josh froze, not wanting to scare them off. "Look at that!" Josh whispered. "I bet we could catch one if we snuck up on them."

Justin said doubtfully, "They can run pretty fast. I've chased them before."

"Let's try anyway. Come on!"

Crouching low, the boys crept forward, freezing every time a turkey looked their way. Their heads were so tiny compared with their bodies that it was hard even to see their eyes.

They made it all the way to the edge of the clearing without alarming the birds. They watched them for a minute, amazed at how big they were. The toms (males) were about four feet long, and stood over three feet tall. These weren't little parakeets, that was for sure! Up close like that they looked mean, like they'd bite.

"Okay, you ready?" Josh whispered. "On the count of three, let's run out and grab one. One . . . two . . . *three!*"

With a mighty leap, the boys burst out of the bushes and ran out into the flock. It caused a sort of turkey explosion. The birds scattered in every direction, flapping their wings and gobble-screaming their heads off. The noise was incredible!

Justin picked a turkey and tried to pounce on it. It took off running, zig-zagging all over the place. Justin zig-zagged after it. When the turkey realized Justin was chasing it, it flapped its wings like crazy and managed to fly up about two feet. It skimmed along over the ground for a short way, then bounced back to the ground. It started running again, its head stretched forward like a roadrunner.

Justin quickly fell behind. Wild turkeys were like poultry rockets once you got them moving. Finally, he gave up and walked back to the clearing.

Josh was waiting for him. "I almost had one," he panted. "But right when I was ready to grab it, it flew off."

Justin laughed. "Mine outran me. He tried to fly, but he couldn't get more than a couple of feet off the ground. Stupid bird!"

"Yeah." Josh shook his head, still trying to catch his breath. It was easier to catch turkeys at the grocery store.

The rest of the weekend wasn't much fun. Justin had to do some chores around the house, and he and Jess got into an argument. It seemed like everyone was grouchy, even little Rachele. Justin began to wish he'd stayed up in the hills with the rattlesnakes.

It was almost a relief to go back to school on Monday. Almost, but not quite. School had been more fun during football season, when he played the offensive line on the Sturgis Williams Middle School Troopers. The season had ended just weeks before.

Justin was looking forward to playing on the high school football team in a few years. He would go straight from being a Sturgis Williams Middle School *Trooper* to a Sturgis Brown High School *Scooper*.

The high school's team mascot was "Scooper

Sam," a big muscular guy with a shovel. He looked like a lumberjack with a flannel shirt and suspenders. The football team's strange name came from an old nickname for the town of Sturgis: "Scooptown." Many years before, when the town was very young, it had consisted mainly of stores. Every payday, the military guys from the nearby Ft. Meade military base came to town to shop. They started calling it "Scooptown" because it scooped up all their money.

Justin's team wasn't great, but they weren't awful, either. They won some and lost some. The Troopers had gotten brand-new football uniforms that year, so at least they *looked* good!

After school that day, Justin walked straight to the VFW Club for boxing practice. Afterward, his dad picked him up.

"How'd it go?" Mr. Hockley asked. "Did you win any rounds?"

It was always more fun talking to his dad about boxing than talking to his mom about it. "Yeah, one or two. Norm says I'm getting better."

"Great!" Mr. Hockley yawned, then smoothed his small mustache. He'd been working nights at the Veteran's Hospital in Ft. Meade, so he hadn't gotten much sleep lately.

"Anything exciting happen at home today?" Justin asked.

His father shook his head. "Just another visit from the furnace company. They came out, took things apart, put them back together again, and said everything looked fine. Then they handed me another big bill."

"Well, *something's* making the house stink. Did they smell it?"

"I don't know. I'm pretty frustrated with them. I'm having the propane company come out on Wednesday to fill our tank. I might ask their guy to look at the furnace. Maybe he'll be able to figure it out."

On Wednesday, Justin had another boxing practice. He spent an hour or two getting beaten up, then went outside to find his mom waiting—anxiously, as usual—in the Ghostbuster.

He got in and sagged tiredly against the seat. The thought of rushing home and into the shower so he could rush to Boy Scouts and *then* rush to church left him even more tired.

"Mom? I think I'm gonna skip Scouts tonight. I just want to relax for a while."

Mrs. Hockley was surprised. "Really? Well, that's up to you. I won't mind taking a break from driving for a few minutes, either." She smiled suddenly. "Tell you what. Since we're not in a rush, do you feel like stopping by Mom's for a milk shake on the way home? We haven't done anything special together for a while. This might be our one chance."

Mom's was a little family restaurant, like a cafe. They made great milk shakes and burgers.

Justin's face lit up. "Are you kidding? Sure, let's go!"

At Mom's they picked a small table and ordered burgers and milk shakes. "Have Dad and Jess and Rachele already eaten?" Justin asked around a bite of hamburger.

Mrs. Hockley looked sheepish. "No. They'll

have to find something around the house for dinner. We don't get to sneak out like this very often. You'd better enjoy it while you can."

"I am!" Justin replied happily. "Thanks, Mom."

After they finished, Mrs. Hockley glanced at her watch. It was her favorite nurse's watch, with a second hand so she could take people's pulses.

"Oh, my goodness!" she exclaimed. "It's 6:15! We'd better get home and get ready for church. Your dad must be wondering what happened to us."

They hurried out to the Ghostbuster. When Mrs. Hockley tried to start it, though, *she* got a surprise. The battery was dead!

"Oh, boy," she fumed. "This is just great. The one time we really need her to start she dies on us. We're going to have to call your father."

Justin grinned. "Ha! You're nailed, Mom."

Mrs. Hockley sighed. "I guess if your dad's coming to fix the Suburban, I should tell him to bring the other kids along. We'd better buy them all dinner. It's going to be too late for church now, too."

A few minutes later, Mr. Hockley showed up with Jess and Rachele. Justin and Mrs. Hockley watched them eat, then went out to jump-start the Suburban. It was almost seven o'clock before they started toward home.

Mr. Hockley unlocked the door and held it open while the rest of the family filed in. As they each stepped inside, they made faces. The oily smell was so strong that they could hardly breathe!

"Del, did you have the propane guy look at the furnace today?" Mrs. Hockley asked. "This is ridiculous. I don't care what the furnace company says. Something's wrong with it!"

"Oh, I meant to tell you. The propane guy said the furnace company put in the wrong "thermal coupler" or something. The part they put in was for a natural gas furnace, not a propane furnace. The guy today put in the right part."

"That's good. But why does it still smell so bad? It's like the smell keeps getting stronger and stronger."

"I don't know. I thought for sure it would be better by tonight." He stretched and rubbed his eyes. "Listen, I'm going to bed. Working that double shift yesterday wore me out. I need some sleep."

Justin changed out of his sweaty boxing clothes, then took his math homework to the kitchen. Mr. Shuck had piled on the homework today. It was going to take at least an hour to finish.

He was spreading out his papers on the kitchen table when Rachele wandered in holding her head. "I don't feel too good," she said. "My head hurts."

Justin tilted back in his chair. "Mom!" he yelled. "Rachele's sick!"

Mrs. Hockley hurried in. "What's the matter, honey?" She felt Rachele's forehead, then shook her head. "You don't feel feverish."

"My head hurts, and I'm sick to my stomach." Rachele's freckled face was suddenly pale. "I think I'm going to throw up."

Justin scooted his chair back, prepared to run

for it. If Rachele started spewing everywhere, he didn't want to be in the line of fire!

"Poor thing," Mrs. Hockley said soothingly. "Come on; I'll get you some Tylenol and put you to bed. You must've caught a virus somewhere."

Justin wrote his name and the date at the top of his paper. Come to think of it, *he* didn't feel so good, either. His head kind of ached, and his neck felt stiff. He massaged the back of his neck for a moment before going back to his homework.

About thirty minutes later, Jess started complaining about a headache and sick stomach. Mrs. Hockley gave him Tylenol and put him to bed. Afterward, she walked into the kitchen where Justin was working.

"There must be a flu bug going around," she said. "I have a headache coming on, too. Are you okay?"

Justin was concentrating on a math problem. "Yeah," he said. "My neck's kind of sore, but that's probably from boxing."

His mom went back out to the living room. Justin worked a few more problems, then decided to check on her. She was being awfully quiet. Maybe she was sick, too.

He found her dozing in a chair in the living room. That was strange; his mom almost never fell asleep in a chair like that. He listened to her breathing for a moment, just to make sure she was alive. She was. He shrugged and went back to his homework.

As he continued to work math problems, though, Justin found it harder and harder to concentrate. *His* head was throbbing now, and his stomach was churning. He told himself it was probably the oily smell in the air. He was determined to finish his homework before he wimped out and went to bed.

He was staring stupidly at a math problem when a little alarm bell went off in his mind. What was making everybody so sick all of a sudden?

Something wasn't right.

I think I'll check on Mom again, he decided, and maybe on Rachele and Jess, too. He rubbed his head, wishing it would stop aching. It was hard to think. It seemed like he'd read about something lately that caused headaches and nausea and drowsiness. What was it?

He scooted his chair back from the table, making a loud scraping noise. His mom usually hated it when he did that, but this time she didn't make a sound. When he walked around the corner into the living room, she was still sprawled in the chair.

Justin hesitated, looking down at her. She was sound asleep, her head lolled sideways. She *never* slept like that. He decided to check her pulse. That was one of the things he'd had to learn to earn his First Aid Merit Badge.

His watch didn't have a second hand, so he'd have to borrow his mom's. He lifted her wrist and tried to gently slide the watch off, but the movement disturbed her. She half-woke and jerked her hand away from him.

"Leave my watch alone," she mumbled irritably.

Somewhat reassured, Justin went back to his homework. If his mom could still yell at him, she couldn't be *too* sick!

But something still nagged at his mind . . . something about sudden headaches and drowsiness. What *was* it? He wished he could remember. He finally got up again, determined this time to take his mother's pulse whether she liked it or not. Something funny was going on.

This time Mrs. Hockley didn't move when he slid off her watch. Justin rubbed his forehead, trying to ignore the throbbing in his head as he reached down to lightly touch her wrist.

He went over the steps in his mind, feeling like he was thinking in slow motion. It was so hard to concentrate! He was tempted to drop onto the couch and take a little nap himself. He could finish his homework later, when he felt better.

No. The sharp thought cut through Justin's drowsiness and confusion. He frowned. What was he doing? Oh, yeah, taking his mom's pulse.

First he had to find her pulse point. Holding the watch up so he could see the second hand, he lightly pressed his three middle fingers—his ring finger, middle finger, and pointer finger—down her wrist, starting at the bottom of her thumb. Sure enough, he could feel the faint pulse beneath his fingertips.

He waited for the watch's second hand to creep back up to the twelve, then started counting. You were supposed to count the heartbeats for exactly thirty seconds, then multiply that number by two to get a pulse rate.

One, two, three, four . . . Justin counted carefully, his eyes glued to his mom's watch. When the second hand hit the six, he had just reached forty-two. That made his mother's pulse an 84.

He let go of her wrist, but didn't move. An average pulse was around eighty, but it was usually lower for someone who was sleeping. He *thought* eighty-four was kind of high, but he wasn't really sure. His First Aid manual said anywhere from sixty to one hundred could be normal.

Chewing his lip, he finally decided to keep his mom's watch and take her pulse again in a few minutes. In the meantime, he wanted to check on everybody else.

He started with Rachele, since she was the littlest. She was a zombie, sleeping so hard that he could've jumped up and down on the bed without waking her. Her pulse was seventy-eight.

Next, he went to Jess's room. His brother mumbled when he touched his wrist, but didn't wake up. His pulse was eighty.

Justin was beginning to think everybody in his family had fast pulse rates while they were asleep. Maybe he was imagining things. Maybe they all just had the flu or something, like his mom said.

Still, he decided to sneak in and check on his dad. He'd gone to bed before everybody else started getting sick, so he might be fine. He didn't move when Justin touched his wrist, but that was probably because he was so tired. His pulse was seventy-two, the lowest of them all.

Justin slowly walked back out to the kitchen, trying to ignore his nagging doubts. He wasn't thinking too clearly. The idea of closing his math books and going to bed sounded better and better.

But something kept him from doing that. It was like a small voice in his mind kept saying, *Don't go to sleep. Something's wrong.* Justin forced himself to stay awake.

He worked on his math for another fifteen minutes, then went out to check on his mom again. This time her pulse was ninety. Alarmed, wondering if he was letting his imagination run wild, Justin trotted down the hall to check on Rachele, Jess, and his dad. His sister and brother's pulses had also increased by seven or eight points. His dad's was about the same, but his skin felt hot to the touch. That was funny, because the room was icy cold.

Back out in the hall, Justin found himself breathing fast. *What was happening?* It didn't make sense. Why would most of his family's pulses go up while they slept?

He wondered again about the smell in the air. Could propane or something be leaking from the furnace? He remembered teasing his mom that their whole house could blow up. Suddenly, it wasn't funny any more. What if their house was full of explosive gas? One small spark would be all it would take!

He didn't realize how long he'd been standing there until he looked at his mother's watch. Ten minutes had passed. He felt sleepy and confused, like he was in the Twilight Zone, or in a bad dream. He had to snap out of it and do something!

I'll check on everybody one more time, he thought. *If their pulses have gone up again, I'll know for sure that something's wrong. Maybe I'm making a big deal out of nothing.*

This time it was harder to take his mom's pulse. It felt like her heart was skipping some beats, but he might be imagining it. His head felt like it was going to explode. He could hardly keep his eyes open.

When he finished counting his mom's heartbeats, though, he wasn't imagining the results. Her pulse had rocketed up to over one hundred! Justin felt a cold prickle of fear. He reached down to shake her.

"Mom!" he said loudly. "Mom, wake up!"

Mrs. Hockley moaned once, but didn't move. Justin shook her shoulder harder, then tried to pull her to her feet. She was limp, like a rag doll. She wouldn't wake up.

Justin ran to the bathroom to get a cold washcloth. He knew from Boy Scouts not to splash water into the face of an unconscious person, because it could get into their lungs. Maybe if he put a damp cloth on her face, it would bring her around.

As he ran the water onto a washcloth, Justin tried to calm himself down. He was supposed to be prepared for most emergencies. He'd been a Boy Scout since he was eight or nine. He knew that the first rule in any crisis was to stay calm.

It was hard to stay calm when your family was dying.

The thought hit Justin with a jolt. Where had that come from? Was that what was happening? He was suddenly afraid. *Please, God, show me what to do,* he prayed as he squeezed out the damp cloth and started back out toward the living room. *Help me help my family!*

He thought furiously about all their symptoms. He knew he'd heard them described before. Where was it? If only he could think clearly!

The furnace. It had to be something to do with the furnace. The smell in the air was stronger than ever. It was doing something to them.

"Mom!" he yelled, putting the cold washcloth on her forehead. "Mom, you've got to wake up!"

Mrs. Hockley moaned softly. Justin grabbed her arm and dragged her to her feet. "You've got to get up. Do you hear me? It's an emergency!"

Mrs. Hockley mumbled something and took one lurching step, then collapsed back into the chair. Justin shook her again, but it was no use. She was out of it.

Justin felt like crying. *What should I do?* he thought again desperately. He needed help!

Then he remembered his dad. The furnace vents were all closed in the back room where he was sleeping. Maybe that was why his pulse wasn't as high as everybody else's. If Justin could wake him up, he could help.

He ran back and shook his father a few times. Mr. Hockley just grunted. Justin got another wet washcloth and put it on his forehead. After three or four more good shakes, Mr. Hockley finally opened his eyes.

Justin got in his face. "Dad, you've got to g-get up quick! Something's wrong with Mom!"

Justin suddenly realized he was stuttering. For some reason, his mouth wasn't working right. He pushed away the frightening thoughts about what that might mean. He couldn't afford to get panicky now!

Mr. Hockley blinked a few times, then sat up. A look of alarm crossed his face as the strong oily smell hit him.

He jumped out of bed. "Where's your mother?"

"In the l-living room," Justin stammered. "I c-can't wake her up."

Mr. Hockley rushed out of the room. Justin went into Rachele's room. His little sister was curled up like a kitten under a thick blanket. He ripped the blanket away and started shaking her.

"Rachele, w-wake up!" he said. "Hurry!"

Her eyes fluttered open. "Leave me alone," she mumbled sleepily.

Justin grabbed her and dragged her to her feet. He might not be able to pick up his mom, but Rachele was a lot smaller. "Stand up!" he ordered, gripping her under both arms. It was like holding up a jellyfish. "C-come on, Rachele, wake up!"

Once he had her standing up by herself, Justin ran into Jess's room. It was easier to wake his brother. "Get up," Justin told him tiredly. It was harder and harder for him to keep his eyes open. "Just d-do it."

Mr. Hockley was out in the living room shaking Mrs. Hockley. When Justin came in, his father looked up. "We've got to get everybody to the hospital. Go get Jess and Rachele up and dressed."

"I already got th-them up. I'll go tell them to get d-dressed."

"Wait!" his father said. "First call Don and ask him to get over here. We need some help!"

Justin's head was pounding so hard that it took him a minute to remember Don Ericsson's phone number. He glanced at the clock. It was almost midnight.

The phone rang twice before a sleepy voice said, "Hello?"

"Don!" Justin exclaimed in relief. "This is J-Justin Hockley, from church. Can you please c-come right over to our house? It's an emergency!"

Don didn't waste any words. "Be right there."

Justin went back to tell Jess and Rachele to get dressed. When he walked back out to the living room, the front door was standing open, letting the icy October air blow in. His father must have opened it.

A few minutes later, Don showed up. He gasped when he stepped in the front door and smelled the thick, oily air. He quickly covered his nose and mouth with his hand.

"What's in here?" he choked.

"The furnace is broken," Mr. Hockley said shortly. "Help me get my wife out of here. She can't walk."

Leaving the door open, Don ran over and

helped carry Mrs. Hockley outside. Justin followed them out to Don's truck, then waited while Don and his dad went back in for Rachele and Jess.

Once they were all outside, Don closed the front door. "I can't believe any of you are still alive after being in there," he said. "I'm taking you straight to the hospital."

Mr. Hockley nodded. "If you can take Justin and Jess in your truck, I'll take my wife and Rachele."

Justin looked over at his father. "A-are you sure you can d-drive, Dad?"

"I'm okay. I don't think I breathed as much of the stuff as the rest of you."

Justin climbed into Don's truck next to Jess. They had only gone a few blocks when Jess started gagging. Don's big fireman's helmet was on the dashboard. He handed it to Jess, who promptly threw up into it.

Justin leaned down, holding his throbbing head in his hands. His chest hurt now with every breath, and his stomach was in knots. He couldn't think clearly.

Only one thought pushed through the haze of pain and confusion. *They were all alive.* Whatever had been killing his family had been stopped just in time.

In the emergency room, doctors strapped oxygen masks onto the Hockleys and drew blood from each of them. The carbon monoxide level in Mr. Hockley's blood was only a little above normal, but the rest of them showed nearly fatal levels. Justin's was the worst.

"I g-guess it's because I ran around a lot, checking on everybody," Justin said from behind his oxygen mask. "I was p-pretty scared, so I was breathing fast."

"Another twenty or thirty minutes in that house and you wouldn't be alive right now," the doctor said bluntly. "You and your family had a very close call."

After the Hockleys were all settled in hospital rooms, their pastor came to visit them. Terry was amazed to hear how close they'd come to dying.

"I hear you're a real hero," he told Justin when he reached his room. "Your dad says you were the one who got everybody out in time."

"I guess," Justin said, embarrassed. "I was so tired th-that I just wanted to fall asleep. I almost did, a couple of times." He added, "Something just kept t-telling me to stay awake, though."

"Is that right?" Terry asked innocently. "What do you think that could've been?"

Justin smiled behind his oxygen mask. "I'm just glad everything t-turned out okay. I'd have hated to have woken up d-dead, especially after spending hours on my math homework. If I'd known I was g-going to die, I could've just skipped it!"

They both laughed.

Jess, Rachele, and Mrs. Hockley were hospitalized overnight, but Justin had to stay in the hospital an extra day. The carbon monoxide he inhaled caused him to have an irregular heartbeat for a while, and left his lungs slightly damaged. It was several days before he could talk without stammering.

Justin was later awarded an Honor Medal for Saving Life by the Boy Scouts of America. He was also presented with an award pin by South Dakota's Governor, George Mickelson, and received a Certificate of Commendation from the Sturgis Volunteer Fire Department.

This story was submitted by reader Steven Morris of Garland, Texas.

Governor Mickelson and Justin at State Capital.

Kids! Have you heard or read about someone who should be a "Real Kid"? We're always looking for new stories for future volumes of *Real Kids, Real Adventures*—true stories about young survivors and heroes. If you've heard about a story that might work, send a newspaper clipping or other information to:

REAL KIDS, REAL ADVENTURES
STORY TIPS
P.O. BOX 461572
GARLAND, TEXAS 75046-1572

You can also e-mail us at: *storytips@realkids.com*. Remember to include your name and phone number in case we need to contact you.

If your story is chosen for use in a future volume of *Real Kids, Real Adventures* (and you were the first one to send that particular story in), you will receive a free, autographed copy of the book and have your name mentioned at the end of the story.

Visit the Real Kids Real Adventures[TM] Web site at:

http://www.realkids.com

Win a free

EUROPEAN ADVENTURE

or a DYNO VFR BIKE!

If you're a "real kid" who loves adventure, this is the contest for you! To enter, just write a story or essay on the subject: "My Greatest Adventure." Winners will be chosen from two age categories: 8–12, and 13–17.

The winner in the 13–17 age category will join other adventurous teens and professional guides for an exciting 21-day summer European adventure, sponsored by Venture Europe. If you win, you'll go white-water rafting and canyoning in France...mountain biking in Italy...backpacking across vast Alpine glaciers and peaks in Switzerland. It'll be three weeks of nonstop adventure!

The winner in the 8–12 age group will win a brand-new Dyno VFR bicycle, complete with a *Real Kids, Real Adventures* helmet, knee pads, and backpack survival kit. If you win, you'll be prepared for adventure wherever you go!

CONTEST RULES:

1. Your story or essay must be 1,000 words or less (or a maximum of four, double-spaced typewritten pages). It can be either fiction or nonfiction. Your entry must include your name, age, birthdate, mailing address, phone number, and the name of your parent(s) or legal guardian. Only *one* entry allowed per person.

2. **The deadline for all entries is April 30th, 1998.** Entries postmarked after April 30th will not be considered, and no entries will be returned. Entries should be mailed to: *Real Kids, Real Adventures Contest*, P.O. Box 461572, Garland, Texas 75046-1572.

3. The winner in the 13–17 age category will receive a free "Ultimate Alps" adventure trip from America's Adventure/Venture Europe. Round-trip airfare to Geneva, Switzerland, to meet the Venture Europe team will be provided from the nearest international airport in the U.S. or Canada.

4. Travel costs for transporting the winner to and from an international airport will be the responsibility of the winner's family. Some physical/legal restrictions apply relating to a winner's participation in the Ultimate Alps adventure. All prizes are nontransferrable. All prizes must be redeemed by **August 1999.**

5. The winner in the 8–12 age category will receive a free Dyno VFR bicycle, complete with a *Real Kids, Real Adventures* helmet, knee pads, and backpack survival kit.

6. This contest is open to all U.S. and Canadian residents ages 8–17. Void where prohibited by law. Sponsored by America's Adventure. The Berkley Publishing Group and its affiliates, successors and assigns are not responsible for any claims or injuries of contestants in connection with the contest or prizes.

America's Adventure, Inc.
2245 Stonecrop Way
Golden, CO 80401-8524, USA
Email: adventur76@aol.com
http://www.realkids.com/AA-VE

Venture Europe
Kerkstraat 34, B9830
Sint-Martens Latem, Belgium, Europe
Email: roelver@pophost.eunet.be